The Stowaway

Nancy Rue

BETHANY HOUSE PUBLISHERS
MINNEAPOLIS, MINNESOTA 55438

A Focus on the Family book published by
Bethany House Publishers
A Ministry of Bethany Fellowship International
11400 Hampshire Avenue South
Minneapolis, Minnesota 55438
www.bethanyhouse.com

Printed in the United States of America by
Bethany Press International, Minneapolis, Minnesota 55438

Library of Congress Cataloging-in-Publication Data

Rue, Nancy N.
    The stowaway / Nancy Rue.
       p. cm. — (Christian heritage series : 2)
    Summary: Spending the summer in Salem Town as the guest of a wealthy ship owner, a ten-year-old Puritan boy asks God for help in dealing with a blackmailing bully.
    ISBN 1-56179-347-7
    [1. Puritans—Fiction. 2. Massachusetts—History—1600-1775—Fiction. 3. Bullies—Fiction. 4. Christian life—Fiction.] I. Title. II. Series: Rue, Nancy N.   Christian heritage series; 2.
PZ7.R88515Sv   1995
[Fic]—dc20   94-41918
                                             CIP
                                             AC

99 00 01 02 03 04 05 / 15 14 13 12 11 10 9 8

For Jim, my favorite sailor

ou'll never get aboard one of Phillip English's ships, Josiah Hutchinson! You'll be lucky even to *see* one!"

"Aye, Josiah! My father says you're going to Salem Town to be schooled—not to become a sailor."

"Josiah Hutchinson—a sailor? Nay—you're going to become a sissy schoolboy!"

The two boys collapsed on the floor, hooting and rolling.

Hope Hutchinson lifted her black, curly head from the group of girls in the corner and hissed at them.

"Get up, you foolish boys! You look like trout flopping on the river bank." She tilted her chin, the way she always did when she took charge. "Let my brother be. What business is it of yours what he does in Salem Town? At least he won't be here—chopping wood and hauling water in the hot sun like the two of you."

She tossed her head back to Sarah Proctor and Rachel

Porter who smiled as if she'd just stunned a pair of crowned princes with those words.

But Josiah Hutchinson glowered at her—the way *he* always did when someone stood up for him before he had a chance to get the words out himself. He turned his sandy-colored head full of wiry curls to Ezekiel Porter and William Proctor who were peeling themselves from the floor and smirking.

"I *am* going to school," he said slowly. "I'm staying with Phillip English, and he's the biggest ship owner in Salem Town. He owns 21 ships—I'm sure to get aboard one of them—sometime . . . ."

His voice trailed off as Ezekiel leaned in close to his face, his huge Porter eyes in sly slits. "The proof then, Josiah."

"Proof?"

"Aye. To prove to us that you've gotten aboard one of Phillip English's ships, you must bring us something—some object—" He looked hard at William Proctor who bobbed his head until his white-blond hair stood up in spikes.

"An—object," Josiah said.

Ezekiel got up and paced the cabin floor, arms crossed importantly. "Aye. The ship's bells or an anchor."

Josiah guffawed. "That—that—shows what you know about ships, Ezekiel Porter. An anchor—an anchor weighs—it weighs—tons!"

Ezekiel stopped pacing and looked at him through narrow slits.

"Then let you show us what *you* know about ships when you come back, eh?" He twitched his eyebrows at William. "We'll be waiting, William and I."

"Can you talk of nothing else?" Hope said from the corner.

Ezekiel strolled toward her with a grin that sliced through both of his sharp cheekbones. "And what are *you* talking about?"

Josiah groaned silently. He couldn't care less what a group of almost-13-year-old girls talked about. It was sure to be something about romance or courting or marriage, and at age almost-11, he'd rather be put into the stocks than listen to it.

The girls, unfortunately, were happy to share.

"We're talking about my cousin, Constance Porter," Ezekiel's sister Rachel said, her eyes Ezekiel-wide.

Sarah Proctor's plump face looked entranced. "She's but 16 years old, and already she's courting!"

"They say she's to be married," Hope put in.

"Married? At 16?" William looked as if his stomach were turning.

"And why shouldn't she?" Hope said. "At 16, boys must pay taxes and serve in the militia. Why shouldn't a girl marry then?"

"Because," Ezekiel said, his eyes twinkling wickedly, "girls—are not boys."

The girls squealed and Hope picked up a basket to swing at him. As Ezekiel dashed to the other side of the cabin to avoid a pummeling by female fists, Josiah blocked them all out and looked sadly around the cabin.

It would be his last time here for a while—for as long as he was in Salem Town, at least. No matter what William and Ezekiel said, it gave him chills to think of spending the summer there. The ships—and the sea—and the sailors rushing around, hauling barrels of cargo on their shoulders. Those thoughts kept him churning in his bed at night, to be away, to see and smell and hear and taste it all.

But other things about going away gave him a lump in his throat, and leaving the cabin—that was one of them. He'd spent some of his happiest hours here. He could still remember the first day he'd come. An Indian boy had carried him here so the widow Faith Hooker could take care of him.

She was different from anyone he'd ever known, the widow. She had time to sit and talk to a ten-year-old boy about things he didn't understand, like hate and fear. She'd made friends with the Indians. Oneko was like her own son, and when she'd introduced him to Josiah, they'd become the kind of friends—who never needed words. No dares and teasing and trying to be better than each other.

Josiah's eyes darted now to Ezekiel and William who were dodging the balls of yarn the girls were tossing at them. He had known Ezekiel and William all of his life. They spent most of their rare free hours together—and there were few for Puritan children in the summer of 1690.

Both the widow and Oneko were gone now—and he missed them. This cabin was all he had left of them. It was a good place to come to be alone when the world started tying itself into knots in his head. Josiah glanced at his five friends, now in a pile in the corner, clawing playfully at each other. He almost wished he and Hope had never told the rest of them about it. It got crowded in here sometimes—like today, when he wanted to say good-bye to it by himself, without Ezekiel's jabbing and Hope's defending him.

Suddenly the pile scattered and everyone—except Hope—stared at the door.

"What? What is it?" she asked.

"Someone knocked!" Sarah whispered.

"What? I can't hear—"

Josiah slipped to Hope's side and said huskily into her ear, "Someone's knocking at the door. What should we do?"

Hope scrambled up and peered out the foggy window. Her face slid into a superior smile.

"It's naught but a beggar woman!" she said. "Josiah, let her in."

"No!" Ezekiel cried. "This is our place!"

"And so it shall remain," Hope said. "Open the door."

Josiah pulled open the rickety wooden door. Squinting in the summer sunlight in front of him was a woman, bent into the shape of a question mark. Thin, no-color hair strung over her shoulders and half hid her twisted face. A chin jutted out to meet her nose. Behind him, Ezekiel snorted.

"Have ye aught to eat?" Her voice screeched like an angry hawk, and Ezekiel screamed with laughter.

"Ye've naught to make fun!" she cawed. She choked on her own voice and finished her sentence by jabbing the air with her stick.

"Hush, Ezekiel!" Rachel said.

Ezekiel plastered his hands over his mouth, but his eyes danced in mirth.

"Come in," Hope said to the beggar. "Josiah, help her in."

The woman's tattered arm looked as if it would fall off if Josiah touched it, but he reached out his hand to guide her inside. She smacked it away with her stick and stumbled in by herself.

The six children formed a wide circle around the woman as she peered through her hair at the inside of the cabin. Her eyes came to rest on the worn shelves beside the fireplace.

"Have you anything to eat?" she asked again.

Everyone looked at Hope.

"She wants to know if we have anything for her to eat," Josiah said to his sister.

"What's the matter? Is she deaf?" the woman screeched in her hawkish voice.

"As a matter of fact she is," Rachel said. "Partly."

"And nay, we have nothing here to eat," Hope told her.

The woman's gray face turned purple and the stick stabbed the air again, nearly knocking Josiah on his backside. "You're liars—every one of ye! How could ye live here without food— ye'd starve!"

"We don't live here!" Ezekiel blurted out.

All eyes turned on him in stony stares. His face went red up to his sharp little cheekbones.

"Idiot," Rachel muttered.

The woman looked from one of them to the other, her faded eyes boring suspiciously into each of them. When she finally spoke, her voice was low and menacing. "If ye don't live here, what are ye doing here?"

"It's our place!" Ezekiel said.

"Shut it!" Rachel said.

Hope took hold of the woman's arm. "This place belongs to a friend of ours," she said smoothly. "She's—away—and we're watchin' over it for her."

"Yes!" Sarah cried and then clapped her hand over her mouth.

"Liars, all of ye!" the woman screamed again.

Hope dug into her basket, pulled out a lump of linen napkin and put it into the woman's hand. "Here," she said, curling the bony fingers around it, "this bread should keep you from fainting dead away before you find a household where they have a real meal for you."

"Aye!" Josiah said suddenly.

Everyone's eyes jerked toward him. Josiah seldom spoke, so to hear him was an event.

"Aye," he said again. "Go you to Thomas Putnam's farm. It's to t'other side of Hathorne's Hill. He always has enough and to spare for—for everyone."

"Hathorne's Hill! I'll be all day walkin' to Hathorne's Hill!" the woman muttered. But she exited and then made her way toward the woods. Inside, the cabin exploded into laughter.

"You sent her to Thomas Putnam's?" Rachel squealed and wrapped her arms around herself.

"Thomas Putnam will drive her off with a hoe and a shovel!" Ezekiel cried.

"Nay! He'll break out his walking stick and they'll stage a duel—right there at his back door!" Hope giggled. "You don't need more schooling, Josiah. You already know what to say when the time comes, eh?"

"Not like some people." Rachel glared at Ezekiel. "'We don't live here!' he tells her! *You* need more schoolin' to teach you when to shut it."

Ezekiel's face was scarlet, and he whirled on Josiah with a forced grin. "At least I won't become a sissy. I can read—some—and I know my numbers. I'll be runnin' the sawmill someday—and you'll be readin' of books and beggin' at the door like that old hag!"

"He won't!" Hope shouted at him.

Ezekiel opened his mouth to return fire, but Josiah didn't wait to hear. He bolted from the cabin and tore into the woods—through the spruce trees and away from the people who talked for him and about him—as if he were stupid.

He slowed to a walk. He wasn't stupid, at least about the ways of things. He knew that from all that had happened in the spring when Hope had had the fever and he had become friends with an Indian boy.

But when it came to school—to reading and figuring and even speaking—that was something different. Every summer from the time he was four until he was seven, he'd gone to dame school at the Porters'. There was no real school in Salem Village, something his father was always angry about, and so the children were taught to read and work with numbers and write their names by someone in the community. Josiah's own father had been well-educated by his father, but times were hard and Papa had no time to work with Josiah. In all those four summers, he'd sweated under Prudence Porter's teaching until the droplets had spilled over onto his primer reader and his hornbook, but he could still barely recite the alphabet or scratch his name on a piece of birch bark with a quill pen. It hadn't escaped the notice of Ezekiel and the others, and they snatched every chance to dangle it in front of him.

But now he was going to Salem Town where Phillip English had offered to put him in a grammar school. Josiah cringed every time he thought of himself sitting at a table with

other smirking boys, stumbling over the simplest words, clawing out big sprawling letters while his hands cramped up into
sweaty balls—

Josiah shook his head. Until now he had managed to blot
out the thought of coming home to his father from Salem
Town in shame because he still couldn't read. All he had to
do was imagine himself aboard one of Phillip English's ships,
perhaps the one that would carry the timber his father and
Ezekiel's father had prepared in the sawmill they owned
together. Just one whiff of the sea air in his imagination, and
the entire alphabet was swept away.

But Ezekiel had put doubts in his mind. What if it were
true that as a "sissy schoolboy" he would never be allowed to
touch a great sail or peek into the hold where the barrels of
molasses nestled for the journey to the West Indies?

If it were true—then he couldn't bring home the proof for
William and Ezekiel. Which meant more teasing—and more
of Hope's standing up and saying, "Let him be!"

"Josiah—wait!" Hope called behind him. "Let you wait
now!"

Josiah slowed his pace to a *crawl*. There was so much to
try and figure out.

✝ ⬥ ✝

Chapter Two

It was a long hot walk from the cabin in Topsfield to their farm in Salem Village. By the time the Porters and Proctors split off to their own homes, Josiah and Hope were dragging their feet on the dusty roads. The sight of their cornfield was more bleak than ever as they passed it.

"Locusts are hateful things," Hope said.

Josiah nodded. He'd spent most of the spring helping his father plant the crop and fertilize it with buckets of smelly dead fish. And just a week ago, a plague of big hungry grasshoppers descended on Salem Village and chewed their corn to ruin.

Hope climbed onto the fence and Josiah joined her.

"At least Papa has the sawmill now," she said. "We've naught to worry that we'll starve."

"And Giles Porter will help Papa this summer while I'm away," Josiah said.

Hope watched his lips as she always did, and then she sniffed. "You know, Josiah, I don't see why you should be the one to be schooled. You don't take to it. You're not stupid— but school things—they pour into you about as fast as cold porridge. That's just the way of it."

She fell silent, but Josiah knew what she was thinking. *She* was the smart one. *She* could read rings around Josiah and leave his head spinning. *She* should go to school, and he should stay and slave in the sun and steaming heat.

But Puritan girls didn't go to school. They had enough to do learning to run a household and raise children. *Huh,* Josiah thought, *why do the girls get all giggly thinking about courting and marriage—when all it means is more work?*

"Crying over your hardship?" said a voice behind them.

Josiah jumped and twisted around. Abigail Williams squinted up at them from the ground, and he nudged Hope. She turned—and frowned.

"Oh," she said in a wooden voice. "It's you."

"Aye," Abigail shouted at her.

Josiah felt his lip curl. Most people in the village were kind to Hope about her half-deafness. But some threw it at her like they were hurling a bad plum, shouting too loud or mouthing their words and forcing Hope to crane forward and strain to hear. The minister's niece, Abigail Williams, and her friends Ann Putnam and Suzanna Walcott were the worst.

But there was no point in Josiah's wrestling Abigail to the ground or anything. Hope could always take care of herself.

Abigail's green eyes narrowed, and she tossed her head toward the ruined corn field. "It's a pity," she said in her too-loud voice.

"Aye," Hope said.

"Of course—you know *why* it happened."

"Locusts," Hope said.

Abigail gave a hard laugh. "But do you know why locusts took *your* cornfield and not the Putnams'?"

"Because the Putnams don't raise corn." Hope smiled slyly at Josiah.

"Nay! Because it's God's punishment on your father!"

"Oh, be gone!" Hope climbed down from the fence, but Abigail caught her arm. She was the same age as Hope but a head taller and, Josiah thought, a head stupider.

"Not before I say this," Abigail yelled into Hope's face. "God is punishing your father because he refuses to support my uncle's ministry. He won't pay taxes for his salary. He won't pay his fines for not coming to Meeting—"

Hope put her hands firmly on Abigail's shoulders and gave her a shake. Abigail's words tumbled helplessly into the air and faded. Hope tilted her chin then and Josiah hung onto the fence. She was about to open fire.

"We go to Meeting in Salem Town," Hope said in a perfectly even voice. "Where the Reverend Higginson preaches about love and joy and peace—unlike your uncle who hollers down at us every Sunday about the bloody fountains and torture chambers of fire that await us when we die if we don't pay his precious salary!" She took a breath and Josiah hung on tighter. "And when it comes to God's punishment—*Abigail*—perhaps He is punishing *you* by giving you a nose so big that it is forever poking into other people's affairs!"

Hope let go of Abigail's shoulders and stepped back.

Abigail stood frozen and then her bully eyes moved slowly to Josiah.

"Have you anything to add?" she asked him.

Josiah shook his head. What more was there to say?

Abigail cackled. "You two make a fine pair. You—" she pointed to Hope, "—the deaf. And you—" she glared back at Josiah, "—you the dumb."

She would have continued cackling until every hen in the village ran to join her, Josiah thought, but a shrill voice behind them chilled them all. The Reverend Parris strode toward them, face pinched and annoyed.

"What's this now?" he said.

Abigail wriggled her shoulders with self-importance. "Uncle, I was only—"

"You were only standing about with idle hands!" he said.

Abigail's face went sulky. Reverend Parris turned sharply toward Hope. "And what are you about?"

Hope lowered her eyes. "Good day, Reverend Parris. We were on our way home to help our father when Abigail stopped to lecture us."

Josiah fought to keep the corners of his mouth from turning up.

Reverend Parris's eyes cut to his niece. "Lecture you?"

"Aye, sir," Hope said. "She was practically preachin' a sermon, right here on the road."

In one swift motion the minister laid hold of Abigail's arm. "Oh, it is a proper preacher now, is it?" he said in a squeezed-tight voice. "You've no time to look after your aunt and your cousin who are both sickly, but you can find hours to gad

about doing my job for me, eh?" He marched off toward the
parsonage with Abigail in tow, ranting about how children are
evil by nature and must be held with a firm hand. But he
remembered Hope and Josiah when he reached the corner
and glanced back over his shoulder to yell, "Go on home with
you now! Idle minds are the devil's workshop."

Abigail looked back, too. Her mouth said nothing, but her
waspish eyes said *I'll get you, Hope Hutchinson. Don't
worry —I'll get you.*

Hope and Josiah were still laughing when they reached
their house, and they both fell into a patch of dandelions at
the edge of the yard to catch their breath.

"You ought to be glad you're leaving town, Josiah," Hope
said as she lay on her back, panting.

"You're in for it with Abigail now."

"Aye." She propped herself up on her elbow. "But you
know, the Reverend Parris was right about one thing."

Josiah's eyebrows shot up. The Hutchinsons rarely thought
the village minister was right about anything. His father said
Samuel Parris was run by the Putnam family—the biggest
fools in Essex County.

"He said idle minds are the devil's workshop," Hope said,
"and that's certainly true for Abigail. With those two servants
doing all the work at the parsonage, she doesn't have enough
to do to keep her out of mischief." Hope chuckled her husky
chuckle. "But that never stopped us, did it, Josiah?"

Josiah stretched out in the bed of dandelions and let the
sun and the memories warm him. He and Hope had had their
share of adventures. Although they seemed to get in trouble

more than stay out of it, their escapes into freedom kept their somber Puritan life from boring them into dull grayness.

"You know, I hate you for going off to school when I have to stay here," Hope said lazily.

Josiah nodded.

"But I shall—"

Josiah sat up suddenly. "Shh!"

"What?" Hope sat up too, and cupped her hand around her ear. Her face twisted with frustration. "What?"

Josiah pointed toward the house and began to crawl closer.

"Josiah—*what?*" Hope wiggled after him on hands and knees until they were crouched under the lead pane windows of the Hutchinson kitchen. Josiah's gray britches blended with the gray clapboards covering the outside of the house, and he listened. Angry voices came in bursts from the windows above them.

"You're breaking down everything we've done to gain independence for Salem Village from Salem Town, Joseph Hutchinson!"

Josiah recognized the voice of Thomas Putnam, the village parish clerk and his father's archenemy.

"Do you like paying taxes to a town that gives you no voice in return? That threatens to seize your land if you don't pay?" said Deacon Edward Putnam, Thomas's brother.

"Israel Porter is our voice," Joseph Hutchinson said in a voice so quiet Hope had to stretch her neck to hear. "He's a Selectman in Salem Town and he speaks for us."

Muttering and mumbling came from the others. Josiah heard Deacon Walcott's voice grumbling with them.

"Like me," Papa went on, "Israel does not find everything that the town demands to be fair to the village. But this village is so scattered in its thinking—there are so many senseless feuds—we are not ready to be independent. We would all be dead in a year without the town to settle our quarrels for us!"

A fist pounded on the table. "Then let you show an interest in the village instead of the town!" Thomas Putnam cried.

"My interest in Salem Town is in my trade with Phillip English," Papa said, "and the church, where my wife and I have been accepted as covenanted members."

Deacon Putnam cleared his throat loudly. Even Hope heard it, and she rolled her eyes at Josiah. "You were not voted into the church here precisely because of that trade you speak of. You cannot go after your own interests at the expense of the society—"

"Stop this!"

The kitchen grew quiet, and Hope and Josiah looked at each other with wide eyes. When their father raised his voice, it was time for everyone to pay careful attention.

"When these colonies were first settled," their father said, "the idea of our fathers was that we be knit together as one man—delight in each other, rejoice together, mourn together, labor and suffer together. That was easy to do then when the land gave us all we needed, and we were all of one mind. But the land no longer gives us our living, and many of us have to look to other means to raise our families and, yes, to support the community—which is *changing*. God has blessed me with more opportunities, and I will take them. As for being of one mind—" Joseph Hutchinson laughed. "I refuse to allow my mind to ever become a narrow, twisted one like yours, Thomas—and Edward—and yours, Walcott. The times are changing, and I will change with them as God wills. Now—good day."

"Hutchinson, I tell you—"

Hope and Josiah squeezed their eyes shut and clung together.

"OUT—OF—MY—HOUSE!" their father roared.

Noise erupted inside—the scraping of chairs, the slamming of doors.

"They comin' out. Run!" Hope gathered herself up from the ground and darted to the side of the house. Josiah waited a second longer, just to see if his father would have to pick one of the Putnams up by his collar and hurl him out the front door—

"See here, Hutchinson!"

Josiah was suddenly grabbed by his own collar. He looked up into the wide, red face of Thomas Putnam. He wiggled to break free, but Goodman Putnam's grip was as tight as his lips.

"Joseph, I've caught your son spying—again! Have your children naught to do but skulk about listening to the conversations of their elders?"

Josiah shrank back as his father appeared on the front step, his big shoulders filling the doorway. His piercing blue eyes looked into Josiah from under his sandy hooded brows. There was no point in lying. There never was. And although his father was a kinder man than any in the village, it still made Josiah's hands clammy to think of disappointing him. Especially in front of the Putnams.

Thomas Putnam gave him a shake. "What will you do about this, Hutchinson?"

"I don't see that that is any of your affair, Mr. Putnam," Papa said. "I think I ordered all of you off my property, did I not?"

Thomas Putnam gave Josiah a final jerk and dropped him to the ground. Turning on his heel, he stomped toward his horse with his brother and Captain Walcott skittering to catch up to him. Joseph Hutchinson stared after them until they'd mounted their horses and galloped away in the dust. Behind him, Josiah silently began to back away.

"Josiah," his father said without turning around. "Stay."

Josiah gulped in air. "I—I'm—I'm sorry—I know it was wrong of me to—"

Papa turned and held up an impatient hand. "None of that now. Come you in with me. I've a letter to write and I want you to deliver it for me straight away."

Without another word he went into the house. Josiah followed him and stood uncertainly in the doorway to the best room. Opposite the entrance hall from the kitchen, this clean, spare room with its shiny wooden rafters and small fireplace was used only for Sundays and special occasions. Papa sat at his writing desk, and his quill pen raced across a piece of parchment. Paper was scarce in Massachusetts, so Josiah knew the message must be an important one.

As his father wrote, Josiah looked around the quiet room. He hadn't spent much time here, but it was once the scene of a very important day in his life. It was the day his father had looked at him and seen someone besides a brainless boy. He felt a pang. He hoped that wouldn't disappear when he went to school—and failed.

"Have you a pouch?" His father stood up and folded the letter.

"Aye, sir." Josiah held out the coarse cloth bag Hope had made for him to replace the leather one he'd given away to a friend so long ago now. His sister had stitched his initials carefully inside. JJH. Josiah Joseph Hutchinson.

"Take you this to Israel Porter's." His father tucked the pouch, now crackling with the letter inside, into Josiah's hand. "Ask for Joseph Putnam and give it to him."

Josiah's eyes widened. *"Joseph—Putnam?"*

"Aye. He's been in Boston since old Putnam died, living with his mother. He's come to Salem Village to claim his inheritance. Be gone with you now!"

Josiah turned slowly, and his father caught his shoulder in one of his big, rough hands. "I've no time to answer your questions now, son. You'll know the answers soon enough, eh?"

"Aye."

The late afternoon sun was bearing down like hot lead as Josiah headed for the bank of the Frost Fish River where Israel Porter's farmhouse stood. He thought about the letter in his pouch.

Joseph Putnam? Why would a Putnam stay at the Porters'? The Porters disliked the Putnams as much as Josiah's family did. And Josiah had never heard of this member of the sprawling Putnam clan of 66 people. He knew Thomas, the parish clerk. Like all the Putnams, he had a big head and a beet-red

face. He was a bitter man, Josiah's father said, because he had
failed in his business ventures, and now his farm was doing
poorly. Edward Putnam was deacon in the Salem Village
Church and seemed to delight in catching the boys whispering during Meeting and popping them on the head with his
stick. And Nathaniel and John who always seemed to be
everywhere, watching and judging and lecturing. Just to be on
the safe side, Josiah broke into a run, down the hill and up to
Israel Porter's front door.

"What are you doing snooping about here, boy?"

Josiah twitched and then broke into a grin.

"Good day to ye, eh?" Giles Porter approached Josiah and
slung a hefty arm around his shoulder. Giles was Ezekiel's
older cousin. He had the large Porter eyes and sharp cheekbones, but he was the handsomest of them all—at least Hope
said so. Josiah admired him because he was strong, but he
had his doubts about Israel Porter's favorite grandson, as well.
Wise old Israel Porter always said none of them should stoop
to the kinds of underhanded pranks the Putnams were fond
of pulling on their enemies. Yet, Josiah had watched Giles
take apart Thomas Putnam's fence one day and put it back
together so that the first person to touch it would knock it
completely down. It bothered Josiah that Giles would do that.
Who had put him up to such a thing?

"Where does your mind go when you get so quiet, eh,
boy?" Giles said to him now.

"I—I don't—"

"Take me with you sometime, eh?" And with a dazzling
grin Giles was gone.

Josiah climbed the front steps and tapped at the door. It was opened by a slender, pretty girl whose Porter eyes glowed blue and soft.

Constance Porter. She was pretty enough, but Josiah still didn't see why all the fuss over courting and marriage—

"Josiah Hutchinson, is it?" Her voice was as soft as her eyes.

Josiah nodded.

"And who would you be wantin' today, Josiah?"

"Well—Joseph—Joseph Putnam. He wouldn't be here, would he?"

Constance's face turned a velvety pink. "Aye. Joseph is here. Would you speak with him?"

Josiah nodded again. *This man must be a saint or something,* he thought. *She talks about him like she's in church.*

Constance disappeared, leaving Josiah standing at the door. He fumbled with the pouch, stood on one foot, then the other, and gazed out over Israel Porter's farm. He was by far the richest man in Salem Village. Many people said Josiah's father was looking to catch up with him. Usually those were the Putnams talking—

"I am Joseph Putnam. What would you have of me, eh?"

Josiah spun around to face the widest grin, the kindest eyes, he'd seen since the Widow Hooker.

This—this was a Putnam?

☩ ☩ ☩

Chapter Three

What—have I grown two noses?" Joseph Putnam said. Josiah pulled his mouth closed. His mother had warned him about gaping at strangers.

"Nay—I—sorry—"

Joseph's eyes were amused. "Have you some business with me, then?"

"Oh—aye!" Josiah thrust forward his pouch.

Joseph took it and looked at it curiously. "You've brought me some sort of cloth bag? Should I thank you?"

"Nay, sir, there's a letter inside—from my father!"

"Now we're getting somewhere!" young Putnam said. "If only I knew who your father was, the entire mystery would be solved."

"Hutchinson!" Josiah sputtered. "Joseph Hutchinson!"

Putnam's eyes were immediately serious. "Would you take the letter out for me, please?"

Josiah fumbled with the string and pawed through the

contents of the pouch—the wooden whistle, some stones—to produce the letter. Joseph Putnam's eyes scanned it quickly, and then they twinkled again as he folded the paper and tucked it inside his waistcoat.

"It seems I'm to pay a visit to your father," he said. "Will you show me the way, young —?"

"Josiah! I'm—I'm Josiah—Hutchinson!"

"Ah, you're Ezekiel's friend, then." Young Putnam grinned down at Josiah. "But I won't take that as a fault until I've gotten to know you. Shall we?"

Dazed, Josiah followed Joseph Putnam across the yard and over Ipswich Road where he took the lead and guided him toward the Hutchinson farm.

"Now then, what questions do you have?" Joseph Putnam said briskly.

"I—questions?"

"It is my experience, Josiah, that boys your age always have questions. But these stiff-necked people here never give you leave to ask them, eh?"

Josiah's answer came slowly. The young man was, after all, a Putnam—and in *his* experience, Putnams couldn't be trusted with the honest questions of ten-year-old boys.

Joseph Putnam nodded. "All right then, your first question is why is a Putnam staying under the roof of the Porters— when everyone knows what devils those Putnams are, eh?"

"Aye," Josiah said carefully.

"I am Thomas's halfbrother."

Josiah frowned.

"What's a halfbrother?" Joseph said. "Ah—lesson number

one in the Putnam family history. Shall I proceed?"

Josiah nodded a little more certainly this time.

"Thomas and Edward and Nathaniel and John's mother died about 25 years ago. You didn't know her then, eh?"

Josiah chuckled.

"Neither did I—and lucky men we are, I understand. They say she was devilish bitter, that one. Had a tongue sharp as an ax and didn't care who she cut with it—sons, husband, anyone. The good Lord took her to her grave, as I said, some 25 years ago. Her husband married again soon after." Joseph laughed. "He was a brave man, wouldn't you say?"

"Aye!"

Joseph sighed. "She is a fair one, his second wife. Martha is her name, and a kinder, softer woman you couldn't ask for. She's one of God's angels, I know it. And do you know how I know it?"

Josiah shook his head.

"She's my mother!" Joseph Putnam grinned as if he were completely pleased with himself. "It was a good match. It gave old Mr. Putnam a new look at life. Even before I was born, he began to see that his sons—my halfbrothers—were made in their mother's mold. Quite honestly," Joseph said as he gave Josiah a wide-eyed look, "he couldn't stand them!"

Joseph Putnam cackled happily and Josiah gazed at him. He couldn't be more than 20 years old and in his fresh, brisk way he was far handsomer than Giles Porter, and from the looks of his clothes, obviously richer than even Israel Porter and certainly smarter than just about anyone Josiah knew, except perhaps his own father. But through it all there was something comfortable about his manner that reminded Josiah once again of the Widow Hooker.

"What happened when your father—when—when he—died?" Josiah said.

"Ah! A question! I knew there would be one!" Joseph Putnam's eyes flickered over Josiah's head, and he put a hand gently on his shoulder. "I shall answer it just as soon as I've gotten this business out of the way."

Josiah followed his gaze to two horses that trotted toward them. Thomas Putnam sat on the back of one and his daughter Ann sat on the other.

"They say if you speak of the devil he shall appear, eh?" Joseph whispered. Then he straightened his fine waistcoat and his shoulders and waited. Josiah tried to make himself invisible at his side.

But Thomas Putnam was not interested in Josiah this time. His eyes bored through his halfbrother as he brought the horse up sharply. Ann, too, ignored him, as she crisply reined in her mare behind her father. Even though small and spidery, she was an excellent rider, as all the Putnams were. Josiah had watched her gallop down Ipswich Road alone at times, unafraid of wolves and Indians and robbers, her wispy hair flying out from under her cap.

"So you've come to collect your inheritance, have you?" Thomas spat out the words at his halfbrother, but Joseph smiled politely.

"Good day, brother. It's been some time, has it not?"

"I am not interested in being pleasant, Joseph. I am interested in the truth."

"Then you shall have it," Joseph said. "What is it you would know of me?"

"It states in my father's will that you shall inherit all but a few acres of his best land here in Salem Village. The remaining sickly property will be divided among Edward, Nathaniel, John and myself."

"It does. Israel Porter showed me that this morning."

Thomas curled his lip. "Israel Porter!"

"Israel Porter is handling the estate, at my mother's request."

"My father was out of his mind when he allowed that!" Thomas sputtered.

"*Our* father was the sanest of all the Putnams," Joseph said calmly. "Thomas, you have asked me nothing yet that you don't already know. What is it that you would have me tell you?"

Thomas held up two fingers. "One—is it not true that you cannot claim the land until you have married?"

"Aye. You know how Father felt about family—"

Thomas cut him off with the raising of the second finger. "Two—have you come to Salem Village then, to marry?"

Joseph began to laugh. Josiah took a step behind him. No one laughed at Thomas Putnam—without an explosion.

Thomas Putnam's big head turned purple from scalp to throat. "You would laugh at me! You're nothing but a boy— with no more brains than this one here!" He pointed an accusing finger at Josiah. Before Josiah could cower behind Joseph's legs, he felt Joseph's hand squeeze his shoulder.

"Leave the boy out of this," Joseph said quietly. "As for my marriage, I am not at liberty to give out that information at this time." He smiled, wisely, Josiah thought. "There is another person involved in such an agreement, is there not?"

Thomas continued to bluster and splutter, and Joseph to talk to him as if he were a small boy having a nightmare. Josiah watched until he became aware that Ann Putnam had edged her horse close to him; the mare's breath was puffing at his neck.

She looked at him, long and hard, *the way a spider must look at a fly before he decides whether to snatch it for his web,* Josiah thought. He squirmed uncomfortably inside his coarse broadcloth shirt. She was a friend to Abigail Williams, that was sure. She had the same threatening way about her, even when she didn't say a word.

Why would anyone want to get married? Josiah said to himself. *Girls are evil—most of them!*

The men continued to argue, and Ann leaned down on her horse's neck as if bored with the wait. As she did, something spilled partway out of her collar and glittered in the sun. Startled, Josiah looked closer.

It was what he thought—a gold chain hung around Ann Putnam's neck. Puritans did not wear jewelry of any kind, not even so much as a hair ribbon. It was rare even to see a piece of lace on a collar because the Puritans felt that adorning the body with shiny trinkets was wicked and evil. A gold necklace on a young girl was almost grounds for putting her in the stocks. Surely her father couldn't know she was wearing it.

"This conversation takes us nowhere, Thomas," Joseph said. "Young Mr. Hutchinson and I must be on our way."

He smiled down at Josiah, but Josiah stayed frozen. He was afraid to draw attention to himself in any way.

He did sneak a glance at Ann as she and her father prepared to ride away. The necklace was tucked safely out of sight, and she stared at Thomas Putnam with rigid eyes.

No, he didn't know about the chain, Josiah decided. And she didn't want him to know—or she would be branded an evil, sinful girl for sure.

When they reached the Hutchinson house, Joseph Hutchinson greeted young Putnam with a smile and a handshake while Josiah stood open-mouthed. He was still stunned that there was a Putnam, a secret Putnam, that his father liked. As the two men went into the best room and closed the door, Josiah watched them wistfully. He would do just about anything to know what they had to talk about, but he didn't dare listen under the window.

Instead he went into the kitchen. Hope stood inside the great fireplace, stirring stew in a pot that hung from the trammel. Beads of sweat dotted her upper lip and curled her black hair even tighter around her cap. Her cheeks were cherry red and her eyes stormy as she glared at Josiah.

"And just where have you been, Mister?"

"I had to deliver a message for Papa—I—you will never guess—who—who the message was for."

"And I have no desire to, either!" she snapped. "Would it trouble you too much to turn the table? We're to have company for supper."

"Joseph Putnam's staying?"

Hope stopped mid-stir and hooted. "A Putnam? At our table? Not likely!"

"Well—this one—this Putnam—"

"There is no *Joseph* Putnam. I'm the one who's deaf, and I don't hear things wrong nearly as much as you do."

"Nay! There is—"

But Hope mopped her forehead with the back of her hand and turned away.

Good, then, Josiah thought, as he turned the tabletop. Hope and her mother used one side for preparing the food, and they used the other side for eating, especially when they had company. And this company Hope could find out about for herself, Josiah decided. No one seemed to believe a thing he said anyway—if they ever let him say it to begin with.

The Hutchinson kitchen was a clean, sparse room made from raw wood and filled with spinning wheels and kettles and the afternoon sun that came in shafts through the diamond-shaped panes of the small windows. It came to life that evening as Joseph Putnam sat at their table and ladled a large helping of stew into his boat-shaped pewter trencher as if it were part of an elegant Boston banquet.

"This spoon meat is as fine as they serve in the wealthiest households, Goody Deborah." He beamed at Josiah's mother, whose face flushed as she smiled down at her trencher.

"I've not laid eyes on you since you were a babe in Martha's arms, Joseph Putnam," she said shyly. Josiah always paid attention when his mother spoke. She talked so seldom—and almost never to a man other than their father.

Young Putnam's eyes flashed to Hope, who stared from

Joseph to her mother and back again. Josiah shot her a look that said clearly, *I told you so.*

"And you are Hope Hutchinson, eh?" Joseph said.

Hope didn't see his lips moving in her direction and kept eating. Josiah nudged her elbow, and she slopped stew onto her apron.

"You'll have to speak up," Papa said. "She's not hearing as well as she did. Had the fever this spring."

"Then I'd best not be mutterin' into my collar, eh, Mistress Hope?" Joseph's voice rang clear in the bare kitchen.

"Aye," Hope said.

"And how old would you be?"

"Thirteen," she said.

Josiah stifled a snort. Hope liked to skip two months to make herself older.

"Ah—time to be thinkin' of the future, eh, Mama?" Joseph smiled at Goody Hutchinson whose eyes softened fondly at Hope.

"She'll make a fine wife," Mama said. "She's finished her sampler and started her chest. There's not much to put in it yet—a few linens—"

Josiah studied the carving on the edge of his trencher without interest. It seemed like all anyone talked about lately was courtship and marriage. It was really too bad that Joseph Putnam was planning to be married. People seemed to get so serious and always be about their work after they set up a household. Young Joseph was more fun than most of the Puritans he knew—at least the adult ones. But that would all change the minute he took a wife and—

"Josiah!"

He jerked in his chair.

"You were asked a question," his father said sharply.

"Aye?"

Joseph Putnam grinned. "'Twas but a trifle, Josiah. Your papa tells me you're to go to school in Salem Town. I only asked if you were looking forward to that, eh?"

"Aye," Josiah said dutifully.

Young Joseph twitched an eyebrow and then turned to Goodman Hutchinson. "And I suppose you've received a fair amount of talk about *that* from my halfbrothers!"

Joseph Hutchinson rolled his eyes. "I'm convinced they have their heads buried in the dirt of their own fields. In 1647—that's 43 years ago now, the Massachusetts General Court passed a law requiring every settlement of 50 families or more to have public schools for their children. We've almost that many Putnam families alone in Salem Village, but it has never happened—and I don't see that it ever will."

"But, Joseph . . . " Young Putnam's bright eyes were teasing. "As long as our children are taught the correct religious doctrine, they will grow up to be good citizens!"

Josiah's father clanged his spoon into his pewter trencher. "Learning is *part* of religion. It represents freedom—freedom to better *know* God! Learning was always respected in these colonies—until now! Now we have people like Thomas Putnam who live in fear that if people learn too much, things will change, and he won't be ready for it."

Joseph Putnam laughed. "Calm yourself, Mister! I was only quoting."

Papa rubbed the back of his neck and smiled a halfsmile. "I know, Joseph. I'm becoming a weary old man. Perhaps with some learning, Josiah can accomplish what I may never see."

"What would that be?" Joseph Putnam asked.

"A wise way of life in this village. One that sees that God wants His people to be happy and prosperous and respectful of each other."

If that is what is expected of me, I might as well give up now, Josiah thought.

"When will he be leaving for Salem Town?" Joseph Putnam said.

"As soon as I can see my way clear to leave the farm and the sawmill."

"I have leave to go there two days hence. Perhaps I could deliver him and a load of your best goods to Phillip English for you."

Josiah's head popped up. Young Putnam's eyes sparkled.

"We would be beholden to you, Joseph," Papa said.

"Good, then. Josiah, you will be ready, eh? Now, Hope Hutchinson. . . " Joseph held up his spoon. "Did you know that in the richest households in Boston, they eat with an instrument called a fork? Two spikes it has—they call them tines—and . . ."

Josiah didn't care about forks. For the moment, he was happy. A trip to Salem Town with young Joseph Putnam was worth all the shame that surely lay ahead.

✝ ⚜ ✝

Chapter Four

The night before he left for Salem Town was a long one for Josiah. The air was smothering in the upstairs room he shared with his sister, and while she slept in the curtained bed next to his cot, Josiah sat in the sluggish breeze stirring through the window. He looked down over the farm and Salem Village.

This was the only home Josiah had ever known, and while there were bickering and harsh people who never seemed to forget anything, Josiah would miss it.

He would miss William and Ezekiel. Ezekiel threw jokes at him like they were rotten apples and laughed when they hit, but the three of them had run together over every inch of Essex County in their ten years. They teased Josiah for being slow to talk, but they also knew he was the best tree climber in the village and the only boy they knew who wasn't afraid of the water. William had once even whispered to him that he knew he could count on him.

But the rough boys at his school in Salem Town—they didn't know those things about him. Would he have to prove himself all over again? What if he failed?

His father had asked him once, "Do you ever *think* about what you're going to do before you do it, Josiah?" It had stung all the way to his center, but Josiah had learned from it, and in time he had shown him that he *did* think.

But that wasn't the kind of thinking he would have to do in school where letters were spread across pages like some kind of puzzle he could never solve. If he came home no smarter than he was now, his father's dream of an educated son who could help change the things that made this village a hard place to live in—that dream would never come true.

Josiah's sigh came from his bare toes. If he had the chance, he knew he could be a good sailor, and that would do his father more good than all the reading in Massachusetts. He could see himself at the helm of some great ship, carrying his father's timber and molasses, selling it all over the world —

His thoughts snapped back to the narrow little window looking down over Salem Village. Ezekiel was probably right. He might never even get to board a ship. He had to turn his efforts to school—and only a miracle from God would make him suceed there.

Closing his eyes, Josiah leaned his forehead against the cool pane and began to pray. Until last spring, God had seemed like some faraway spirit that the Reverend Parris prayed to at Meeting. But as he came to know his father better, Josiah learned that God was actually a Friend, and then the Widow Hooker had brought Him even closer. Now Josiah believed that as long as he was good, he could ask God for anything.

Father, can you please make a miracle happen?

Hope was cleaning the kitchen floor with sand the next morning when Josiah brought the bundle of belongings his mother had put together for him downstairs where he would wait for Joseph Putnam. She looked up from her bucket with a red, flustered face.

"You're off, then," she said, her voice knotted.

"Aye—soon."

"Well, well, well." She fanned out a scattering of sand on the floor and attacked it savagely with a rag.

Josiah chewed at his lip. "Well—what?"

"While I am here, cleaning this floor with sand from the beaches of Salem Town, *you* shall be on those very beaches—standing in it!" She flung another half bucket of the white powder, covering the toes of Josiah's boots.

"You talk—you talk as if—I were going to lie about—eating from a fork!" Josiah cried. "If you want to—to—go to school instead of me—you're welcome to it! Go on and say it. Everyone knows you're sma—smarter than I am."

He hadn't meant to say all that, and his face burned. Hope sat up on her knees and tilted her head. Her eyes softened.

"You're frightened, then?" she said.

Josiah felt the tears pricking at his eyes and he blinked fast.

"This is silly, Josiah!" She flung her rag to the floor. "You're not stupid! You must just try very hard. And pray—do you pray?"

"Aye."

She slid across the wooden planks and wiped the sand from his boots. "Then, while you're about it, pray for me."

"You! Oh—aye—who will be your ears for you, eh?"

She waved her hand impatiently. "No, not that. It's Abigail Williams and Ann Putnam I've got business with, eh? They'll try to get back at me for what I did to Abigail in front of her uncle the other day. I'll be needin' your prayers for that!"

Josiah nodded. But as he looked at Hope, her eyes bright with confidence, her cheeks shining with life, he knew she'd handle anything that came along.

"Ah—a proper gentlemen already, is he?" said a voice from the doorway. "You've not even left the village and you have your sister wipin' your boots for you!"

Joseph Putnam strode into the room, and to Josiah even the sun slanting across the table suddenly seemed brighter.

"You're ready then, young Hutchinson?" Putnam said.

"Aye."

"Let you take your bag out to the wagon then. You're father's loaded it already. I must ask Mistress Hutchinson to pour me a cup of cider before we're off."

As Josiah stepped into the narrow hallway, his bag slung over his back, his father appeared in the doorway to the best room.

"Come here, son."

Josiah followed him to the trestle table that stood polished and graceful in front of the window. His father had taken the Bible out of its wooden box, and it lay open in the light. With reverent fingers his father stroked the pages.

"Sixty years ago in England," he said, "my father and other Puritans were not allowed to read this book at their Meetings because it was against the law of the Church of England. I am often judged by the men in this town for reading about the thoughts and discoveries of men in other books, but I still consider this the most important book, and here in Massachusetts we are all free to enjoy it."

Josiah nodded.

"It is a sacred treasure, and that is why no one in a household is allowed to touch it until he is able to read it." He looked at Josiah from under his sandy eyebrows. "Nothing would make me more proud than for you to come home from Salem Town and hold this book in your hands and read from it to this family." Slowly, he closed the book and brushed his hand across Josiah's back. "Let you be off, then."

Josiah was glad when Joseph Putnam's wagon, loaded with goods and covered with a heavy cloth, pulled off down the road from the farm. There was hope in his father's eyes and tears in his mother's—and the tears that threatened to roll down his own cheeks were more than he wanted anyone to see. As Salem Village passed by—Hadlock's Bridge over Crane Brook, the Porter/Hutchinson sawmill, the marshy Endicott farm, and the shops and taverns that lined the Ipswich Road—an unfamiliar feeling took hold in the pit of his stomach. It felt like a sick kind of fear and sounded in his mind like voices calling him back—back home. It became harder to hold back the tears, and so Josiah sat quietly beside Joseph Putnam and watched his village fall behind him in a blur.

He had been to Salem Town many times. His family went to Meeting there every Sunday. But he had never gone without them. And never before had he felt the burden of coming back to them a different person. Someone they could be proud of.

"I visited your father's sawmill this morning," young Putnam said after a while. "Those great wheels were a churnin' and a 'turnin'.." He slipped a glance sideways at Josiah. "Just like the ones in your head now, eh?"

Josiah shrugged and mumbled, "Aye, sir."

"It's to be expected, you know," he went on. "It's a great load they've put on you. I'll warrant you've much to think about. You can lighten your load by talkin' of it—though it's caught my ear that you don't talk much."

"Aye—nay." Josiah shook his confused head and fell silent.

"D'you mind if I chat a bit, then?" Joseph said. "I've a few things in my head that need sortin' out."

Josiah shook his head.

Joseph slowed the horses a little and leaned back comfortably on his seat as if he were sitting in Josiah's kitchen. "Do you know aught about women, Josiah?"

Josiah choked.

"Nor do you want to, I see," Joseph said, laughing.

"No—it's just—they twist my thoughts around."

Joseph's laughter turned to a roar, and he threw his head back to let it bellow from his throat.

"You've summed up the pain of a thousand years of male suffering, my good man!" he cried. "I think I'll keep you around me."

He brought his head up to wipe his eyes and at once

became serious. He pointed his finger down the Ipswich Road. "Do you know this fellow?"

Josiah peered through the dust at a figure fast approaching on a horse from the direction of Salem Town. Josiah couldn't see his face, but from the way the rider's tall, thin body leaned over the horse's mane, Josiah could tell he was in a hurry. The animal's hooves dug and tore at the dusty road in spite of the thick summer heat.

As he drew nearer, the rider yanked on the reins and the horse pulled up and danced in their path. Joseph pulled his own horses to a halt and stood up in the wagon, one hand shielding his eyes from the sun.

"Can we help you?" Joseph called to the horseman.

Instead of answering, the rider pulled his hat lower over his eyes and climbed from his horse. Only when he came up to the side of the wagon did Josiah see that all of his face except his eyes was covered with a white napkin, and that the hair beneath his hat was tucked into one, too. Joseph saw it, as well, and smiled.

"It's a good idea, that covering on your face," he said. "Keeps the dust out of your nose, eh?"

"Nay," said the man in a muffled voice. "It keeps you from seeing who I am. Down from that wagon, now, both of ye." He reached inside his dusty greatcoat and pulled out a wooden club with a spiked end.

In a frozen moment, every bee in the woods seemed to stop buzzing and Josiah's brain stopped thinking. Then the horseman slammed the club against the side of the wagon and broke the freeze.

"Down, I say!"

Josiah threw one leg over the side of the wagon, but Joseph grabbed his arm and held on. "Nay, son—this man has no authority over us."

He has a club, Josiah thought. *That's authority enough for me!*

Once again, the masked rider slammed his weapon against the wagon. Josiah held on to keep from falling off, one leg still straddling its side.

"You're naught but a bully!" Joseph said. "What is it you want?"

"Whatever you have in that wagon."

"You can't have it. It isn't yours. Anything else before we are on our way?"

In one smooth motion the horseman raised his club with one hand and clenched his fist around Josiah's arm with the other. With one jerk Josiah was on the ground, looking up at the spikes of the club swinging over his head. With one blow his skull would shatter.

✜ ⬥ ✜

Chapter Five

𝕴'll have what's in the wagon, or this stick goes through your boy's head, eh?"

The man's voice was gruff and rattled, like stones bouncing in a clay jar.

"Aye—the boy's worth more than the goods," Joseph said. "Leave him be and come take your fill."

The masked horseman lowered the club, but he kept a vise grip on Josiah's arm and dragged him along to the back of the wagon. Something hard dug into Josiah's flesh. Joseph Putnam pulled back the heavy cloth cover Goodman Hutchinson had so carefully spread over his kegs of molasses, his bundles of salted meat, his neat rows of cut timber and barrel hoops and shingles. A lump clogged Josiah's throat as he thought of how hard his father had worked for this wagon load of goods—and how his eyes would sink deeper under his hooded brows when they told him they had traded it for Josiah's safety.

The horseman gave a jeering laugh from under his mask. "This is your treasure? Why, I see 20 times more than this every day!"

"Then you won't be wanting this measly affair." Joseph Putnam smiled at the man, but Josiah saw no twinkle in his eyes. "Now if you'll let loose of the boy, we shall be out of your way."

"Take it out," the horseman ordered.

"What do you say?"

"I say take it out! All of it!"

Joseph Putnam laughed stiffly. "And what will you do with it? Carry it all off on horseback?"

"What I do with it is my affair! Take it out, I say!"

The robber's fingers dug deeper into Josiah's arm and once again he felt something hard cut at his skin. That and the way the man's eyes glittered above his mask kept him from trying to tear free. He kept his terrified eyes on Joseph Putnam, who was nodding calmly.

"Good, then," he said. "You shall have every scrap and tittle of it."

Josiah's insides churned as Joseph hiked himself up onto the back of the wagon and with two hands lifted out a small barrel of molasses. With the keg high over his head he turned, and cried, "Josiah! Run!"

The keg was suspended in air for a split second and then came crashing toward them. With a curse, the masked horseman let go of him and dodged. Josiah scrambled under the wagon.

"You're a bloody mongrel!" the horseman screamed as the keg hit the ground.

"Aye, I'm that and more!" Joseph screamed back.

Cowering behind a rear wheel, Josiah saw only pounding fists and thrusting feet as the two men wrapped themselves around each other and splattered the ground with their sweat and spit. Sweat began to pour down his own face, and his heart pounded above all sounds—until a scream from the masked man punctured the air.

"Get in the wagon, Josiah!" Joseph shouted. "Where are you? Get in!"

Josiah caught a glimpse of the masked horseman rolling in a ball toward the road and then saw Joseph's boots clump by. When the wagon squeaked with his weight, Josiah tumbled out from under it.

But as he did, the wagon rolled forward. The wheel caught his sleeve and bore down over his arm, pressing his flesh against its rim.

Slowly, as if he were in his own nightmare, the wheel rolled forward, pinching his skin with ripping pain. When at last it finished its turn Josiah clutched his arm to himself and moaned.

"Josiah!" Joseph called, his voice frantic. "Josiah! Where are you!"

"Here!" Josiah scrambled up, holding his arm against him.

But his words were cut off as a wiry hand closed over his mouth. Another hand fell clumsily over his eyes, and Josiah caught sight of a heavy gold ring, a squiggle engraved on it. Josiah chomped down as hard as he could on the hand covering his mouth. Almost before his teeth had sunk all the way into the man's flesh, the hands pulled away and Josiah tore into the dust toward the wagon. Joseph Putnam's arm reached down and yanked him up by his free hand, banging

Josiah's knees against the side as he tumbled in. Josiah fell backward against the seat and caught one more look through the dust. The masked horseman was on his knees, clutching his belly with one hand and massaging the other with his lips.

Joseph snapped his whip over the horses' heads and the wagon careened down Ipswich Road. Josiah's heart was hammering its way out of his chest, and his arm was throbbing, the blood seeping through his broadcloth shirt.

Joseph saw it, too, and he clutched Josiah's shoulder.

"You're hurt! How badly, lad?"

Josiah pulled back his sleeve, and his stomach turned over. Blood spurted from a gaping opening and torn flesh curled away from it.

"I don't want to stop here for fear our friend will catch up with us again!" Joseph held the reins in one hand and peeled off his gray waistcoat with the other. "Here—wrap this 'round it and lie down in the bottom of the wagon."

Josiah hesitated. He had never held any cloth so fine in his hand. *And I'm to soak this with blood?* he thought.

"We've naught but a short ways to go," Joseph said. "There will be help for you at the English house."

Josiah twisted the smooth coat around his arm and lay back. He could almost feel his face turning white. But as he looked up at Joseph Putnam, a laugh bubbled up inside. The fine young man still sat tall in the wagon seat, ordering the horses on like a prince. But his oak-colored hair flew out in tatters, as did his shirt and the legs of his britches. One side of his noble face was smeared with dirt—and it occurred to Josiah that he was having a wonderful time.

As if reading his mind, Joseph looked down at him and grinned.

"Bit him, did you, lad?" he shouted over the pounding of the hooves.

"Aye!"

"Would I had thought of that. I got him in the stomach, though, with my knee. It didn't do any serious damage—just slowed him down a little." He laughed into the wind. "We're a team, eh?"

Josiah grinned back and nodded. He wished Joseph was staying in Salem Town with him.

When they arrived in front of Phillip English's mansion on Essex Street in Salem Town, the words that Josiah was hurt were hardly out of Joseph's mouth before Josiah was whisked out of the wagon. Two servants carried him upstairs and propped him up on a mountain of cushions in a high bed with embroidered curtains tossing in the breeze that wafted in from the harbor.

Mrs. English and a woman called Ruth bathed his face and his wound and put a pewter mug of cider in one hand and one of springwater beside him. Josiah was relieved when they left and Joseph came in, his face washed and his clothes changed. He helped Josiah slip out of his clothes and into a linen nightshirt.

"But I'm not s—I'm—I'm not sick!" Josiah whispered to him.

"You've had more of a tumble than you know," Joseph said. "You'll barely be able to walk tomorrow. Let's have a look."

Together they took stock of the hard marks on Josiah's

arms and legs. At the same time, their eyes locked on one on his upper arm. It was perfectly square and appeared to have a letter in the center.

"What's this now?" Joseph said. "An 'S'?"

A picture of a heavy gold ring appeared in Josiah's mind. It had dug into his arm for a long time, and he had seen it just before he'd sunk his teeth into the masked horseman's hand.

"Will we need a doctor for that arm?" said Phillip English from the doorway.

"No!" Josiah cried, and then sank lower under the eider-down quilt. Mr. English hadn't really spoken to him, and Josiah was sure he hadn't expected him to give the orders. Quickly, for a reason he couldn't name, Josiah covered the sign of the S on his arm.

"Why no doctor, Josiah?" Joseph said gently.

"Because—it's—it's naught but a—but a small cut."

"These hearty villagers, eh, Joseph?" Phillip English said. "That gash is big enough to store a handful of schillings!"

Joseph nodded solemnly as he examined Josiah's arm. The blood had been washed away, but the skin was fiery red and swollen, and the wound gaped like an angry mouth. Perhaps doctors were better here in the town, Josiah thought, but he would never want the village physician, Dr. Griggs, to touch him. He carried foul-smelling and worse-tasting medicines in his pouch, and he was always ready to give up on a limb—or even a person. He'd told them last spring that Hope was as good as dead, and then the widow—

Josiah sat up cautiously. "Would you—if you could make—a poultice of bruised comfrey root—that would close the wound. And then boil the rest for broth—I would drink that."

Phillip and Joseph looked at each other and, seeming to find no other answer there, both nodded.

"Comfrey roots it is! I shall tell the cook!" Phillip English tapped his walking stick, as if that would magically make the cure appear.

Josiah remembered the walking stick from the first time he'd met his host, last spring when the Hutchinsons had begun to attend Meeting here in the town. It was sleek and rich-looking, made of beech with an ivory handle and gold trim. As he swung it at his side, it gently reminded everyone that he was the wealthiest shipowner in town.

But as he leaned over the bed to give Josiah's shoulder a tap, Josiah saw something else beautiful and rich-looking hanging from Mr. English's neck. It was a gold chain, and on the end of it dangled what appeared to be a whistle. But it was nothing like the wooden whistle Josiah carried in the cloth pouch at his waist. This was long and slender and looked as if it were made of pure gold. Along its side were six tiny, sparkling stones, the likes of which Josiah had never seen before. He could only guess that they were jewels.

He had certainly seen his share of fine jewelry lately. Ann Putnam's gold chain. The robber's gold ring. And now this elegant whistle. He had never seen Phillip English wear it before because he had only seen him on Sundays. No Puritan—whether born into the church or converted to it, like Mr. English—would dare wear so fine a gold piece to Meeting.

"Did either of you get a look at this robber?" Mr. English was saying.

"I didn't," Joseph Putnam said. "He wore a mask, and even his hair was covered by a scarf and then a hat. I'm certain he was disguising his voice as well."

Mr. English shook his head thoughtfully. "I wonder if he is in any way connected with the thieves who are robbing me."

"You!"

"Aye. I've had a number of things stolen from the warehouse and some of the ships. Not in large quantities, but certainly valuable—and small enough to be carried away by someone on horseback."

Joseph Putnam laughed. "If it was the same thief, he was in over his head this time. He could never have gotten away with all of Joseph Hutchinson's goods before we were back to grab him." He turned to Josiah. "He was no match for us, eh, lad?"

Phillip English smiled. "I only thank God you made it here," he said and left.

"Where did you learn that cure you asked for?" Joseph said when he was gone. "Certainly not from old Dr. Griggs!"

"Nay." Josiah squirmed under the hot quilt. "I learned it from a friend—and she—she—the Indians taught it to her."

Joseph grinned and, for the first time since the robber had appeared, his eyes twinkled. "Ah, Josiah, you're a lad I want close to me at all times. You know things that would make the likes of Thomas Putnam shiver in their boots! Now. . . ."

He swept back the quilt. "You may not die from the wound, but you will from the heat if you let these people smother you."

Josiah sighed and wiggled his toes in the brisk air that parted his bed curtains. Although his window faced the harbor, he couldn't see the ships from his bed, but with a sniff, he took in the smell—the salt and the codfish. That was enough for now.

Joseph chuckled. "Let you grow accustomed to this luxury, Josiah, for this is how you'll live these next weeks—and especially since you're a wounded man, eh?"

Josiah lay there that night and listened to the sounds of the harbor—the sea gulls crying out tired good nights, the sea slapping against the docks, and the thick lines creaking as they held their ships in port. It wasn't Salem Village, but the blur of the day's events racing through his brain—and the effects of the comfrey-root tea—took away the sick longing for home in his stomach and finally lulled him away.

When he awoke, the bed curtains were bright with sunlight beating on them; he could feel it was well into afternoon. He bolted upright on his pile of cushions and then gasped. Pain pulsed through every muscle, and he fell back, breathing hard.

"Goo' day," said a tiny voice at his elbow.

Josiah looked down to see a face as small as the voice that spoke. Large brown eyes shone up at him like two shiny schillings.

"Good—good day," he said back.

The curtain was tugged and another little round face peeked in. This one had a mouth too small to talk, but it sprang open in a toothless smile.

"Josiah Hutchinson, meet Judith and Hannah English," said still another voice. Josiah knew this one belonged to Mary English. He tried again to sit up.

"It's late—I know—I didn't mean—I shouldn't have slept so long—"

She laughed, a clear tinkling laugh that made her two babies chirp with her like little birds. "We expected you to sleep on into tomorrow if you'd a mind to. The girls and I have only come to see if you are in need of anything." She leaned in as if she had some magic secret, and Josiah found himself craning forward a little, too, to catch it. "You must take delight in this time," she whispered. "You may never know another like it."

She gathered the two babies against her and swept from the room like their graceful bird mother. "But get you well soon," she said over her shoulder. "My husband looks forward to a boy in the house."

In the two days that followed, Josiah did take delight. He was not allowed to move from his plush curtained throne as servants piled the soft mounds of comfrey poultice on his arm three times a day. They soothed his feverish neck with cool cloths until both he and the cut looked healthy again. The strange imprint of the gold ring faded from his arm, although the memory remained engraved in his mind.

Each afternoon, Mary English came into his room when the baby birds were sleeping and read to him in her clear, sweet voice. It was unusual for a New England woman to be able to read, and Josiah got up the courage to ask her about it one day. It led to a discovery that made him want to scurry back to Salem Village—right then.

"You—you must be very—very well-ed—educated," he said to her.

"Aye. In England," she said, "my father believed it was important for all of his children, both boys and girls, to be able to read." She patted his leg that lay comfortably under a cool linen sheet. "And you will do the same, very soon, Josiah. The Reverend Nicholas Noyes has a difficult program, I understand, but you seem a bright boy—"

"Nich—Nicholas Noyes?"

"Aye. He is the teacher of the grammar school. It isn't uncommon for the minister of the town to teach the boys—" She stopped, her ivory forehead wrinkled. "What is it, Josiah? Is something wrong?"

Something was very wrong. Reverend Nicholas Noyes was the assistant minister of the church in Salem Town. Josiah had come across him the very first Sunday he had come here with his family—and he would rather move into the barn with a bull than ever have to meet him again. Unlike Reverend Higginson, Reverend Noyes was an impatient, overstuffed man who seldom smiled and never waited to hear the whole story before he placed blame—usually on the children. Why was it, Josiah had asked himself many times, that God allowed people who seemed to hate children to become His ministers? Even now he could feel the pinch of Reverend Noyes's fingers on his ear as he had that Sunday—and now he would go to the school where he was the teacher? Josiah shuddered, and the sick longing came back into his stomach. Not only would he have the rough town boys laughing at him as he struggled over primer and quill pen, but he would surely have the reverend plucking him up by the scruff of the neck and tossing him into the corner three or four times a day.

"Josiah, what is it?" Mary English said again.

"I—I don't—fe—feel very well."

Mrs. English sent at once for a tray of sweets, her favorite remedy for most of Josiah's ills. Since he had been here, he had feasted every day on treats he usually saw once a year at Thanksgiving or a wedding. For a while, they did help chase away the thought of cowering under Reverend Noyes's rod. Candied orange peel and sweet cakes with caraway seeds, dried fruits and raisins, almonds and chocolate—and some wonder he had no name for that melted in his mouth.

"Macaroons," Joseph Putnam told him on Saturday afternoon, his mouth stuffed with two. "These are really the medicine that made you well, as I see it. You're allowed up tomorrow, and if you feel fit, you can go to Meeting."

Josiah popped another macaroon into his mouth and nodded. It was more pampering than he was sure Reverend Parris's niece and daughter got, and this morning he'd begun to think it would feel good to be out from behind these curtains. The thought of Hope picking onions in the sizzling heat while he bulged his stomach with sugary tidbits made it hard for him to enjoy himself. Besides, he was ready to see the ships at least, and that had for the moment crowded out the thought that on Monday, it would be time to begin school with Reverend Noyes—and time for Joseph Putnam to return to Salem Village.

A mist hung softly over the harbor on the morning of the Sabbath as the English family, Joseph Putnam, and Josiah walked up the hill to the Church of Christ at Salem Town.

Phillip swung his elegant walking stick, and Mary swished her skirts, the lacy edges brushing the dust. Hope would be gazing at her forbidden finery about now. The fanciest thing she owned was a petticoat with Bible verses embroidered on it. But Josiah looked longingly back at the harbor where the ships still slept under their silken sheet of fog. As he craned to see them, his foot hit a rock and he stumbled against Joseph.

"Are you certain he's strong enough to make this walk?" Mary English said to her husband.

Josiah watched closely for Phillip English's answer. His own quiet mother would never question his father's decisions about anything. This was a world with different rules.

"He is hearty, are you not, lad?" Mr. English said.

Josiah nodded and tried to watch where he was going.

"'Twould be a pity to miss the Meeting, what with your family being there, eh?" Joseph Putnam said.

Josiah's head came up. Of course. With all the excitement and special attention, he'd forgotten that he would see them —Papa and Mama and Hope—when they came to town for church. He sighed. He had only been gone from home a few days, but already he missed them. Perhaps he should simply go home with them now—and let Hope be the one to make their father proud. It would probably work out that way anyway, now that he knew who his teacher was.

The Hutchinsons were already seated in the Meeting House when they arrived. Mama sat on the east side of the church with Hope beside her. Their seats were behind the oldest inhabitants of Salem Town and the government and military officials. They sat in front of the paid servants and the slaves and those who didn't contribute as much to the society as his father did.

Across from Mama, on the west side, sat Joseph Hutchinson, his large shoulders looking square and proud in his cinnamon-colored coat. Josiah would be able to watch them all from his usual place in the boys' pew in the high gallery at the back of the Meeting House.

Boys, the deacons always said, were an unruly bunch and needed to be separated from the rest of the congregation so their foolish pranks wouldn't upset the worship service. Josiah himself had noticed that putting all the boys together made tricks easier to pull off. Even though the deacon watched like a hungry hawk for whispering and games so he could poke the young criminals with his long pole, a clever team of even two or three boys could get away with spitting pumpkin seeds at the young girls below or setting loose a frog when the sermon droned on past three hours.

It had been several months since Josiah had joined in a prank at Meeting in Salem Village with William and Ezekiel. When the Parish committee had refused to elect Joseph and Deborah Hutchinson into church membership, they had begun to make the long trip to town to worship with Reverend Higginson. And in this church, Josiah didn't dare so much as fall asleep during prayer.

These were a different breed, these town boys. William and Ezekiel and even the Putnam boys were full of mischief, but their capers never hurt anyone. Here, his very first day, a tall, redheaded boy had wrestled him to the ground and Reverend Noyes had blamed the entire fight on Josiah.

So as he always did on Sunday mornings, Josiah found a spot at the end of the back row of the gallery and tried to make himself invisible. He would meet up with all of them in school soon enough.

Down the row the boys shuffled their feet and squirmed in their places and hissed to each other. The deacon jabbed his pole like he would a sword as he poked their backs and spat out "SHH!"

All at once, Josiah felt himself being grabbed by the back of the collar. His seat came off the bench, and he shivered as a pain shot down his injured arm.

"You, boy!" the deacon said hotly in his ear. "You sit among these mongrels and see if separating them doesn't do some good in keeping them quiet."

With a mighty shove he moved the boys in the center of the bench apart with his pole and dropped Josiah into the space. They rocked against him from both sides.

"Now, then," the deacon said hoarsely, "quiet here."

Josiah didn't dare look at them. The hostile eyes of all the boys drilled through the top of his head, as though he'd asked to be placed there like a turkey among wolves.

A voice beside him made him jerk his head up in fear. "It's *you*!"

Josiah found himself staring into the colorless eyes of the redheaded boy.

✝ ✞ ✝

Chapter Six

For the blink of a moment, a startled look flashed through the redhead's eyes. But before Josiah could even give it a name, it was replaced by a slow smirk.

Noiselessly, the boy's mouth formed the taunting words, "Farm boy."

The redhead jabbed the boy on the other side of him with his elbow, and that boy, too, leaned in to give Josiah a jeering smile. Instantly, it seemed, every boy on both sides of him slanted forward to laugh with their eyes. Josiah just stared at the heads of the boys in the row in front of him.

The only thing Josiah knew for sure about the Salem Town boys was that there seemed to be two groups of them. The tall, redheaded boy, who looked perhaps 14, was the leader of one gang. A stocky blond with shoulders as big as Josiah's father's led the other. Hope had told him once that she'd found out the blond boy was only 12, in spite of what his overgrown body looked like. That same hulk of a boy sat in front of him now.

Suddenly, the entire congregation was on its feet and Josiah with them. Reverend Higginson must be making his way to the front of the Meeting House, although Josiah couldn't see anything from behind the shoulders in front of him. The congregation said a long prayer, and then the deacon led them in a psalm from the Bay Psalm Book. Around him the boys pretended to recite along, but their lips moved in gibberish as they continued to wiggle their eyebrows at him and stick out their tongues. Josiah kept stony still.

When they were seated for Reverend Higginson's sermon, Josiah tried to listen. The old minister's retelling of the Bible stories and his preaching about the kindness and blessings of the Lord always made Josiah feel peaceful. It reminded him of how the Widow Hooker had talked about God, as if He were very near. Reverend Parris seemed to drive Him to the furthest corners of the earth.

But today he found it impossible to keep his mind on what the preacher was saying. On one side, the redhead kept his finger poised at Josiah's ribs, and each time the deacon turned his attention to the minister below, he stuck him in the side. He still had a bruise there from slamming against the side of the wagon, and he had to bite his lip now to keep from yipping with pain.

On the other side, the boys passed something from the end of the row toward the center where Josiah sat. He didn't dare turn to look right at them, but out of the corner of his eye he saw that whatever it was, it was small and alive, and it didn't want to be handed from one grimy cupped set of palms to the other.

Two boys down it almost got away and three of them lunged for it, which brought the deacon scurrying from his corner, pole poised for a poke. Everyone turned into a statue, and Josiah was probably the most still of all. But the deacon scowled at him as if the entire outburst were his fault, and he'd better do something to correct it in a hurry.

When the deacon returned to his seat, the hands came out again, and the terrified little whatever-it-was ended up in the palm of the boy next to Josiah. The boy looked across Josiah to the redhead for instructions. The leader smiled wickedly and nodded toward the stocky blond boy in front of them.

Josiah held his breath to keep from gasping out loud. Pressing his hands together as tightly as he dared, the boy on his right positioned them at the back of the blond boy's collar and dumped his moving treasure down the boy's shirt.

Every hand in his row covered a mouth as the boys bent over with smothered laughter. The blond boy let out a squeak and came straight up off the bench, dancing and clawing at the back of his shirt. The deacon bolted from his corner, and two of the blond's friends yanked him down into his seat. With one final spasm he freed his shirt from his britches, and a shiny black cricket hopped frantically onto the floor.

The deacon's eyes bulged as he glowered down the row in front of them. With one smooth swoop, the red-haired boy scooped up the cricket, laid Josiah's palms flat, and deposited it between them. He was holding both of Josiah's hands in his fist when the deacon bore down on their row.

"Let's have it!" he hissed through his teeth.

There was a frenzy of shrugging and waving of empty palms, and Josiah strained to get his free so he could let the cricket go. But his muscles were sore and weak, and he was still holding the bug when the red-haired boy raised his other hand and pointed self-righteously at Josiah.

With a swift crack the pole came down on Josiah's hands— just as the redhead pulled his away. Josiah's palms flew apart and the cricket made a mad hop for the floor. With pain stinging his hands and tears stinging his eyes, Josiah stared after it, wishing with everything in him that he could hop away with it.

In the church below, Reverend Higginson purred on about God's grace while in the gallery, the deacon stuck his rod inside Josiah's shirt collar and lifted him from the seat like a fish at the end of a pole. He dropped him at the end of the row and with his foot rolled him down to his corner at the front of the gallery.

"Suffer the little children to come unto me," Reverend Higginson said below. "Jesus tells us we must have the faith of a child—"

Josiah Hutchinson sat in a crumpled heap on the floor and bit back his tears. Even if he were allowed to stay, how could he survive among these wretched boys?

"Mr. Hutchinson!" the deacon barked across the church-yard at the end of the Meeting. "Mr. Hutchinson!" Without waiting for him to turn around, the deacon marched toward Papa, towing Josiah behind him, his fingers pinching his shoulder blade.

Joseph Hutchinson stood with old Israel Porter and Joseph Putnam. When he turned around, Josiah squeezed his eyes shut. His father hadn't seen him in nearly a week, and now his first sight of him would be this. If he could have pulled away from the pinching fingers, he would have—and run as fast and as far as he could.

"What's this now?" his father said.

Phillip English stepped up beside him. "Good heavens! The boy is already injured! Leave him be, deacon!"

"And I trust his father will 'injure' him more when he knows what the boy has done—right there in the Lord's house, while Reverend Higginson himself was preaching His Word!"

A small crowd had gathered by now. Josiah saw his mother, clutching her hands in front of her, and Hope beside her, shaking her head. The blond boy and his group formed a knot in the back, and the redhead and his followers skulked behind a tree. Other church members moved in curiously, and through them puffy Reverend Nicholas Noyes pushed his way, red-faced and muttering. Josiah prayed for a hole to open in the churchyard so he could fall into it.

"Here, here!" Reverend Noyes cried. "What monstrous thing —" His tiny eyes fell on Josiah and then rolled back in his head. "It's this fellow again, is it?"

"'Again'?" Phillip English said. "Forgive me, Joseph, but I brought the boy here and I must speak for him."

"Aye," Papa said.

Phillip English's voice was calm, but he waved his walking stick impatiently at Reverend Noyes. "What do you mean 'again'?"

"Why, the very first time this boy darkened the door of this church, he brought trouble here among the boys! And now today, I understand he put a cricket down young Hollingsworth's back—during Meeting!"

A chorus of chortles rose from the blond boy's group, and the redhead's group fell into a pile to keep from exploding.

"I'm afraid you're mistaken, Reverend Noyes," Phillip said.

"I beg your pardon!"

"Since Josiah Hutchinson came to my house several days ago, he has been in bed recovering from injuries he received during a robbery on the Ipswich Road. This morning is the first time he has been in a position to catch a cricket, and that would have been on our walk to Meeting—and I assure you, he did not!"

The rest of the churchyard seemed satisfied with that explanation and turned back to talk of hot weather and puddings. But Reverend Noyes was growing redder and more bloated by the minute, and Josiah held his breath and watched him.

"That may be, Mr. English," the reverend finally said. "But if you are planning to put this boy in my school, as I understand you are, I suggest you change your plans immediately. There is trouble wherever he goes. He is not welcome."

The minister took a gasping breath and waddled off angrily. The deacon sprinted after him, scattering both groups of boys with his pole.

Josiah didn't know which way to look, even when his mother came to him and pulled him into a hug against her skirts. There was a squeamish silence until Joseph Putnam's clear laugh burst out.

"We've naught to worry that things will be dull with Josiah about, have we?" he said. "I must say, you're a brave lad to have chosen that big brute as your target. He's twice your size and then some!"

"But I didn't—" Josiah cried.

"Of course you didn't." Phillip English nudged Papa lightly with his walking stick. "I'm for sorting this all out over dinner. What say you?"

Papa hadn't said a word yet, nor had he looked at Josiah. He nodded now, and he, Phillip, Israel, and Joseph headed down the hill toward the mansion on Essex Street. Mary English took Mama's arm and followed them.

"Well, come on, then," Hope said to Josiah.

They trudged along in silence for a while. Josiah never felt like talking much, and right now he saw no use in even trying. The words would have stuck in the lump clogging his throat.

"Why didn't you tell them you didn't do it?" Hope said finally.

Josiah shrugged.

"You *didn't* do it, did you?"

"No!"

"Ah, then you *can* talk. Why didn't you tell them?"

"When did they ever give me a chance?"

Hope stomped her foot as she walked. "I'd have made them listen, had it been me."

"Well, it wasn't you," Josiah said stubbornly. "It was me."

"And why is it always you, Josiah?"

Josiah looked at her quickly. "What do you mean?"

"You do seem to draw trouble like molasses draws flies,

even if you don't actually do anything wrong yourself."

Josiah hung his head miserably.

"There is your answer," she said.

"Where?"

She put her hand under his chin and snapped it up.
"There." And she stomped off to catch up with the women.

Although dinner was a banquet of meats and vegetables—
eaten with forks—and topped with an array of apple, mince,
and dried-berry pies, spice cakes with maple sugar frosting,
and candied fruits and nuts, it all tasted like wet leaves to
Josiah as he waited for the hatchet to fall on him. His father
still hadn't said a word to him, and his deep-set, piercing eyes
looked into him now from across the table. Josiah had
thought the days of disappointing his father were gone. But it
seemed they'd returned like a bad dream.

"Who is this Hollingsworth?" Joseph Putnam selected a
macaroon from the pile of treats on the table and snuck a
wink at Josiah.

"Captain Hollingsworth owns a fleet of ships that he builds
and sends to sea from Salem Harbor," Phillip English said.

"He's your rival then?"

"He needn't be. There's plenty of business for all of us, the
way this port is growing. But he's made himself so, yes."

Young Putnam's eyes twinkled with interest. "For what
reason?"

Phillip English tilted his elegant head. "Jealousy, perhaps?
It seems my ships last longer and don't meet with as many
fatal accidents as his."

"Providence!" Israel Porter said, laughing.

"I don't doubt God has His hand in it," Phillip English said. "Hollingsworth is a scoundrel. But I know for certain it has much to do with the timber he uses to build his ships. It's all green wood and handled by shipwrights who know only what they learn as they go at the expense of many a sailor's life. If he would only allow the wood to season before he begins building . . . but he wants to build overnight what has taken me years. I've tried to share what I've learned, but Captain Hollingsworth is a stubborn man—and a foolish one, too." He chuckled. "I'm afraid young Josiah got caught in the middle of it this morning."

Josiah looked up, startled.

"Ach!" Papa said.

"Hear me out, Joseph," Phillip English said quietly. "That burly, yellow-haired lad who claims Josiah put a cricket down his back is Captain Hollingsworth's son, Nathan. He leads an ill-mannered bunch of boys, many of whom work for Hollingsworth. They carry this imagined rivalry between my company and his wherever they go." He looked at Josiah. "Was there a red-haired boy nearby when this happened in Meeting?"

Josiah said nothing. Hope jabbed him hard in the rib.

"He—he was right—be—beside me," Josiah muttered. He stopped, and Hope let fly with another sharp poke.

"It was he who—he put the cricket in my hand when it cr—crawled out of the boy's shirt. I—I—I hadn't time to—to let it go—before the deacon—"

"You see, Hutchinson, the boy hadn't a prayer. The

red-haired boy and his friends will jump at any chance to make the Hollingsworth crowd look foolish—without getting caught themselves, of course. It gives them an excuse to get into mischief."

"Why didn't you come forward with this before, boy?" Israel Porter said.

"And who would have believed him?" It was the first Joseph Putnam had spoken in several minutes, and his usually merry voice was serious.

An uncomfortable silence followed as if they were somehow waiting for Josiah to clear it all up for them. Papa's blue eyes looked into Josiah.

"He's a quiet one, that one," Joseph Hutchinson said. "I daresay he'd have spoken up if he thought his or someone else's life depended on it. That's what it takes for the boy to speak."

Everyone nodded, though with puzzled faces. Only Joseph Putnam smiled at him.

"I'd thought to send him to school," Papa went on, "in hopes that learning would give him the tools to bring forth what goes on in that mind."

"Aye," Joseph Putnam said softly.

"It looks as if you've drowned that possibility," Israel Porter said. "And that may be God's blessing even so. I wouldn't send my grandson to be taught by the likes of Nicholas Noyes. But, then—" He shook his head. "He is the only school-master in town."

Old Israel was right, and for a moment Josiah hated him for it. The next words out of his father's mouth were sure to

be, "I guess we have naught to do but take him home, then."
It was what a secret part of him wished for—but at this
moment he would rather hear his death sentence.

But it was Joseph Putnam who spoke next. "In Boston
where I grew up, there are many learned men, and it is not
uncommon for families to send their sons to their kinsmen
there to receive their educations privately. I myself was
schooled alone by the Mather family."

Papa gave a hard laugh. "I'm to send him to Boston now?"

"There is no need to." Joseph Putnam's face broke into a
splendid smile. "Boston is here."

"You, Joseph?" Israel Porter said.

"I can think of no better. I have naught to do but wait for
my affairs to be settled in Salem Village, in more ways than
one. If you would have me, Phillip, I could stay here several
days a week and teach Josiah."

Josiah kept his eyes on Joseph Putnam's shining face. He
was afraid if he looked at anyone else he would see doubts
and reasons why-not and laughter at such an idea. He wanted,
just for the moment, to believe it could be true.

"I couldn't pay for that," Papa said gruffly.

"How were you to pay for Reverend Noyes's school?"
Joseph Putnam asked.

"It was part of our business agreement," English said.

"And why might I not be a part of that same agreement?"

"Young Putnam *is* brilliant," Israel Porter said, "for all he
comes from some of the same seed as that ignorant brood in
Salem Village."

Phillip English looked at Papa. "He is your son, Joseph,

and by rights it's your decision. But I have no quarrel with the plan and would indeed be delighted to have Putnam here under my roof."

"As would I," Mary English agreed.

Mama smiled gratefully at her, and Mary English gently squeezed her arm. With frightened eyes, Josiah turned back to his father. It was indeed in his hands now.

Beneath the table, Hope kicked at his foot. Did she want him to say something? Surely not. He already felt like he was sitting in a place so fragile it would shatter if he even breathed. When she kicked him again, he shot her a look. She nodded hard toward Papa.

Josiah turned to find his father looking deep into him. Josiah knew as always that he would come out knowing something—something right and wise. *Please, God,* Josiah prayed, *let it be something right and wise—and what I want, too.*

"Very well, then," his father said. "But—with this as the sticking point, and I hold you all as my witnesses—if there is another bit of trouble, even the size of a walnut-shell full, Josiah comes home and the schooling is done. Agreed?"

All heads nodded, except Joseph Putnam's. His eyes clouded, and for one horrible moment Josiah thought he was about to disagree and crumble the dream into a thousand pieces. And then his eye caught Josiah's. Almost without moving, Josiah shook his head.

Joseph Putnam nodded and put on a smile. "Good, then! I shall return to Salem Village tonight to put a few affairs in order and gather my belongings, and we shall commence with the education of young Josiah Hutchinson the day after next."

A cloud seemed to lift from over the table then. Sweets were passed, and talk turned to timber prices, high tides, and the recent robberies. At his place, Josiah let out the breath he had stored up all morning, and when no one was looking, he stuffed two macaroons into his mouth.

☩ ⸙ ☩

Chapter Seven

Josiah was used to waking up early on the farm. By the time the sun came up, he had the wood chopped, the cows milked, the chickens fed, and the oxen watered.

But since he'd arrived in Salem Town, he had slept far into the morning every day. So the day after the Sabbath, he knew he must be well—his eyes sprang open even before the misty gray light could crack through the curtains.

He got up, dressed, and crept mouselike downstairs. It was strangely silent in the house, as if all the Englishes were still asleep. At his house, a person only stayed in bed past dawn if there was hard sickness—and even then the crops and the sawmill were still tended to.

In the kitchen, Ruth and the cook slipped around on tiptoe, and even the fire seemed to crackle more softly than most did. Josiah watched as the cook pulled a loaf of bread from the baking alcove in the big brick fireplace. He took a long breath in to smell it, and the cook, round-faced and round-bodied, grinned. Her teeth were like a row of dried berries, but the smile was a happy one. And Josiah liked to be smiled at.

"Hungry, are you, Master Josiah?"

Josiah nodded.

"'Tis a pity I have none of those macaroons you love so well for your breakfast. But let me show you where they're kept." She waddled over to a large cupboard by the window where she opened the doors to reveal a number of dishes with linen napkins draped neatly over them to keep their contents fresh. "I usually bake the macaroons after dinner, so if you come down of an afternoon, you just help yourself."

"Is it—some sort of holiday?" Josiah asked.

Cook arched an eyebrow. "Why, no, lad. Mrs. English always insists there be plenty of good food about. She doesn't believe people can be at their best when they're starved for comfort. Says that's why Mr. English is so successful. That and the good Lord's blessing, of course."

Josiah mumbled, "Of course," then watched her close the cupboard full of treasures. Ezekiel and William would never believe this.

The door to the outside swung open and Phillip English came in. He was in his shirt sleeves but, as always, the gleaming gold and white walking stick hung at his side, and he wore the jeweled whistle around his neck. Josiah couldn't help staring at it. It was truly the finest thing he had ever seen.

"You're up early, eh?" Mr. English said.

"Aye, sir."

"You're ready, then, for a bit of a tour this morning?"

"A—tour?" Josiah's heart sped up, but he didn't dare hope—

"I've a mind to check on my newest ship. She's just come back from her first voyage, and I'd like to see how she fared. Since you won't be starting school until tomorrow, perhaps you'd like to join me, eh?"

Josiah felt his eyes bulging, but he managed to nod. "We're to go—we're to go—*aboard* the ship, sir?"

The corners of Phillip English's mouth twitched. "Aye."

"Will you be wanting breakfast before you go, Mr. English?" Cook asked.

But Josiah already stood at the open door, his hat in his hand.

Mr. English laughed and shook his head. "It appears that I won't."

The day was breaking brisk and clear as Phillip English and Josiah walked along Essex Street to the east. Even though Josiah's thoughts were headed for the sea like bullets toward a target, he did notice the grand houses that lined Essex Street on either side. Some of them were three stories high, and all had glass windows and fine stately lines. They made the square, brown houses in Salem Village look like poor second cousins.

At the end of the street, where it ran into Shallop Cove, they turned right to head toward the harbor, and soon they reached a narrow neck of land that led toward the sea. Josiah took a sniff of the salty, fish-flavored air and closed his eyes with pleasure. You could barely smell it as far away as the Meeting House, but here a gentle wind blew it warmly toward him. He could fill his whole head with it and with the image of the ships and the sailors—

He felt a nudge at his shoulder. The shiny walking stick tapped him gently, then pointed to the right. "There is the harbor, then," Phillip English said.

As easily as that, the imagined ships came into view. There before him was Salem Harbor.

Ship after ship rocked along the protected wharf below him, their bows tipping gracefully above the water. Josiah had never seen such a sight—and yet it was everything his mind had painted.

Noble masts pointed importantly to the sky. Sailors scurried back and forth with kegs on their shoulders or coils of rope over their arms. Lines creaked with weight, and water sloshed against the hulls, and every inch of the harbor below him bustled with the business of the sea. He could barely breathe at the sight of it all, the sight he'd waited so long to see.

Phillip English chuckled softly. "The General Court did us a great favor a while back. They ordered that all goods shipped in or out of the colony had to pass through Boston— or Salem. That is, of course, as it should be. She's a fine natural harbor with a network of rivers feeding into her. A blessing for men like me." He turned to go. "Shall we, then?"

Josiah tore his eyes from the harbor and followed Mr. English. Before them lay a huge piece of land that would have been an island if it wasn't connected to shore by the narrow strip they were passing on. And then they came upon the biggest building he had ever seen. Its giant doors were thrown open, and it was bulging with crates and bags and barrels.

"This is my warehouse," Phillip English said. "It provides safekeeping for the cargo when we're waiting to load it aboard the ships, or holding it when we bring it in. I've a mind to ship every kind of goods the people of the world ask for—except slaves." His face darkened for a minute, but then he straightened his shoulders. "I own 13 other buildings in Salem Town, but this one is by far the biggest."

Josiah mouthed the number 13 to try to understand just how wealthy Phillip English really was. He was too overwhelmed to speak out loud.

"Some of those goods you see in there now are going to the other colonies—Savannah and Charleston and Norfolk and such. The rest is bound for the Caribbean." He pointed out past the harbor.

Josiah nodded as if he knew where that was.

"We'll take them the usual dried and pickled cod and mackerel, flour, peas, beef, pork, and, for the first time, barrel staves and hoops and shingles and boards. The people in the West Indies have almost no lumber products—and you know where those came from, eh?"

"Aye—I think so."

"Your father is a wise man, Josiah," Phillip English said. "He sees that the shipping business is turning the Massachusetts colony from a scattered collection of farming communities like Salem Village into a place that will make the world take notice. And he knows it can help farmers like

himself rise above their poverty. God is providing the chance
to do more than just survive, and he's taking that chance."
Phillip English shook his elegant head until his shiny hair
shivered over his shoulders. "'Tis a pity men like the Putnams
tell him he's ungodly to want to be prosperous. God wants His
people to be happy, eh?"

Josiah had never quite thought of it that way, but now as
they left the warehouse behind, it did occur to him that the
people who seemed the most comfortable with God—the
Widow Hooker, Reverend Higginson, and Joseph Putnam—
were also the happiest people he knew.

"We'll walk along my wharf and see how the shipbuilding
goes, eh?" Mr. English said. "This should be of special interest to you, Josiah."

"Why?" Josiah managed to say.

"You shall see presently."

They continued past the great warehouse and walked along
the rocky coast that was teeming with activity. The shouting
of the sailors, the pounding of pegs, the constant movement
of the sea created a racket that, to Josiah, was music. He had
an urge to shout just to be a part of it—although what he
would shout, he didn't have the first clue.

Every man who passed said good morning to Phillip
English and doffed his sailor's cap. Phillip English knew them
all by name, and some he even stopped to chat with.

"How be the wife?" he would ask. Or, "So you have a new
son now, eh? Does he look to be a sailor some 20 years
hence, eh?"

Some of the workers who scurried around them didn't look

much older than himself, Josiah thought. The forbidden idea that he might forget about book learning and farming and come here to the wharf to learn his living crept back into his mind. Only remembering that Joseph Putnam was his teacher made him push the thought aside. Still, if he could chop wood and drive a team of oxen, as he did at home, surely he could hike a barrel onto his shoulder or handle those great ropes that held the ships snugly at their docks—

"There she is!" Phillip English cried out.

Josiah looked up to where the walking stick pointed. There on the wharf was the almost-finished form of a ship—so close that with only a few steps, Josiah could touch it.

"Come on, then," Phillip English said. "Let's have a closer look, eh?"

As if he were walking in a dream, Josiah followed him.

High up on a cradle of wood the mighty ship towered over them. She stretched so long, Josiah knew it would take over a hundred steps to get from the front to the back. One end, which curved up toward the sky, was at least three stories high, while the other was two. In between, three tall poles stretched up, waiting for the sails that would soon flap from them.

She was as elegant as Phillip English himself. Josiah had watched ships move up the rivers from time to time, but compared to this beauty, they were like the leaf boats he and Hope used to make to "sail" in the brooks when they were little. Josiah held his breath in her presence. Thoughts of standing on her deck, riding the waves out to sea, crowded into his mind.

"She's something of a galleon," Phillip English said. "Like

a Spanish ship. Not like anything they've seen here in New England."

"Nay," Josiah said.

"There are but a handful of trained shipwrights—those are shipbuilders—in the colony, but I've managed to find most of them. The man who builds this vessel is a Spaniard. Juan speaks barely a word of English, but he builds a beautiful ship, eh? That's what comes of trading with France and Portugal and Spain—places Captain Hollingsworth is afraid to go."

Josiah could only nod. Phillip English tossed out words like "lateen-rigged" and "mizzenmast" and "spritsail," which all sounded like bird mutterings to Josiah, and so he was about to slip back into the dream of himself as ship's captain when he was jolted back to the present.

"In a small way, this is your ship, too, Josiah," Phillip English said. "The timber that went into the making of this vessel came from your father's sawmill. Without his business, I could not have created this magnificent craft."

Josiah's eyes sprang open so wide, he was sure they'd pop out and bounce onto the ground. Phillip English brushed his shoulder with his fingertips. "You've a right to be proud of her."

They walked slowly around the vessel. Phillip eyed her carefully, running his fingers over the sides, and when they reached the other side, a small, wiry man looked up from the tool he was sliding over the wood. Josiah had watched his father use a planer when building furniture. This man was obviously smoothing the surface of the ship. *So she will be perfect,* Josiah thought.

When he saw Phillip English, the man put down the planer

and hurried over. Even standing up, he had a curved look to him. His crow-black hair was tied at the base of his neck, and when he smiled at his master, Josiah saw a sparse assortment of well-used teeth.

"Aye, she's a beauty, Juan!" Phillip English said.

Juan bobbed his head happily as Josiah stared. *This* man was the builder of this grand vessel? He looked like some of the beggars who came to their door in Salem Village groveling for food!

"My friend, Josiah Hutchinson," Mr. English said. "You know his father, Joseph, of course?"

Again Juan bounced his black head up and down and beamed even brighter. Josiah knew right away this man liked his father. A person of few words himself, he could read people's faces the way other people read words.

"Josiah will be about all summer," Phillip English told Juan. "I thought you should know who he is, lest you mistake him for one of Hollingsworth's boys and run him into the sea, eh?"

Juan scowled playfully and nodded at Josiah. Josiah nodded back.

Phillip English said good-bye to Juan and led the way farther out into the harbor, along a rocky section that he called the Point of Rocks. Stretching out from the jagged coast like perfectly spaced fingers were twenty wooden docks. Josiah counted them quickly. Each one had a large building at the end that thrust into the water. Josiah's heart, which had tried to pound its way out of his chest ever since he'd caught sight of the harbor, sank a little. Only a few of the docks had ships swaying at their sides.

"Most of my fleet is out to sea now," Phillip English said. "This is the best time of year for transporting goods. Let's go have a look at the *Adventure*, though. She's just returned from her maiden voyage. I've a mind to inspect her."

Josiah felt every footstep that led him to the ship and registered every breath of wind and cry of a sea gull. He didn't want to forget a single detail of something he'd waited for ever since he could remember. But he tried to listen to Phillip English, who talked easily as they made their way past the empty docks and down the wharf.

"The *Adventure* is a ketch," he told Josiah. "You'll notice she's a good deal smaller than our new galleon back there, though she is but one journey old herself."

As they drew closer, Josiah began to drink in the *Adventure*. There were only two masts, one taller than the other, and Josiah counted four sails folded tightly around them by a web of lines he longed to know the names of. She didn't have the magnificent beauty of the newer galleon, but she looked sturdy and strong and proud. Josiah smiled as he rolled the words "ketch" and "galleon" around in his mind. William and Ezekiel had said he wouldn't learn aught about ships, but already the magic names were part of his language.

"The ketch is most useful for my West Indian trade," Phillip English said. "Ah—see there. They're unloading her cargo now."

Josiah felt a delicious shiver as he watched the sailors emerge one by one from the bowels of the ship, laden like oxen with bundles and packages in mysterious shapes. As they drew nearer, Phillip English fell silent while he studied their burdens and sized up his ship. Josiah imagined their contents—the things Phillip English said he brought in from the Indies. Perhaps there was sugar in that one and cloth in that. And maybe that one was a barrel of nails or oil or salt—

"Look out there, boy!" a voice shouted above the rest. "Are ye an idiot? Clear the way!"

The shouts came so rapidly—like angry sparks from a runaway fire—it took Josiah a full five seconds to realize he was about to be run over by a huge rolling barrel. And pushing it from behind with a stick was a long-legged boy with very red hair.

✢ ✢ ✢

Chapter Eight

The red-haired boy gave the barrel one more push, and it spun toward Josiah as if it, too, wanted to bowl him over. Josiah jumped out of the way, and the boy tore past after the runaway keg, sneering at Josiah as he went.

"So it's you again, is it, farm boy?" the boy called over his shoulder.

"Simon!"

Both boys looked behind them. Simon stopped the barrel with his stick and waited. Phillip English strode toward them, and for the first time, Josiah saw anger in his eyes.

"Sorry, sir," Simon said in a voice that sounded less sorry than any Josiah had ever heard.

"What are you about here? Josiah Hutchinson is a guest on our wharf. You have naught to try to run him over with a barrel of molasses, eh?"

"Nay, sir." Simon's face went slack, and his lower lip hung like a loose stocking.

"Go on, then, and be about your business," Phillip English said. "And see that cargo hold is clean before she's loaded up again."

"Aye, sir." Simon's own eyes were flashing anger as he turned and rolled his barrel of molasses away.

"Don't judge all of my men by that one," Phillip English said. "He's a scoundrel, that. But he's an orphan. I hate to turn him out on the streets."

As they walked toward the *Adventure*, Josiah knew he should feel sorry for poor orphan Simon, but that was impossible when poor orphan Simon had made trouble for him every time he'd seen him. His father had said one more occurrence and he would be sent home. He'd have to stay out of Simon's way.

As soon as they stepped onto the dock that led to the ketch, all thoughts of Simon were swept away. Josiah took a deep breath. He was going aboard a ship.

A small bridge stretched from the dock to the *Adventure*. The large barrels and packages were lowered over the side, but busy sailors carried the smaller cargo items over this bridge, and even Phillip English waited for them to pass before leading Josiah onto it. He followed quickly, so as not to do anything to keep him from actually setting foot aboard the vessel, but he did sneak a peek over the side. It wasn't like crossing Crane Brook over Hadlock's Bridge at all. He squeezed his arm to make sure it was really happening.

"You've just crossed the gangplank, Josiah," Phillip English said. "Welcome aboard the *Adventure*."

Josiah got out, "Thank you, sir."

A sailor in a bright blue coat, who was watching them as they crossed, now grasped the whistle that hung around his neck by a ribbon and gave it a toot. Grinning like a boy, Phillip English took hold of the jeweled whistle that hung around his own neck and blew back.

The sailor laughed. "That's a beautiful boatswain's pipe, Mr. English. It puts mine to shame, eh?"

A boatswain's pipe. He had pronounced it "bow-sun," and Josiah rolled the word around in his mind. He knew what it was called now, and in a moment he knew what it was for. Every time the blue-coated sailor blew a signal, the men around him knew what to do, without his ever having to say a word. It wasn't much different than what he and William and Ezekiel did with their wooden whistles. Perhaps that was why no Puritan questioned Mr. English's wearing his sparkling gold one—because it had a purpose.

"I bought it from a Portuguese ship's captain when last I sailed there," Phillip English said. "I told him I wasn't a captain, or even a boatswain, but he said a ship owner was a dignitary of the sea and must have one." He laughed. "It's naught but a lark for me. You're the one should have it, using one the way you do."

The sailor shook his head. "I wouldn't want so rich a thing hangin' round my neck, sir. The way things are around this wharf, I'd be killed while it was stolen from me." His face clouded. "I would be careful, Mr. English, sir."

"So I shall," he said. "And now let me introduce my young friend, Josiah Hutchinson."

"Ah—Hutchinson," the sailor said. "That's becoming a familiar name 'round here. Welcome aboard!"

Josiah barely had time to thank him before he and Mr. English were off again, and both his mind and his eyes were racing over everything around him. He tried to listen as Phillip English gave the names to the mysterious lines and ladders and fastenings. But there was so much to learn—and it was all as magical as Josiah had imagined.

They stood first on a deck at the front of the ship. It was, he learned, the forecastle deck. Phillip English pronounced it "focksul." Josiah leaned over the railing and imagined the ship bound for shore and land coming into view.

From there they walked briskly about the ship. Phillip English inspected every inch of his craft, remembering to give Josiah a piece of information now and then.

The capstan looked like a big drum and lowered the thick ropes that dropped the heavy cargo over the side. The hawser was the line reserved for the anchor. Josiah laughed as he remembered Ezekiel Porter daring him to bring it home. A rope ladder hung over the side, leading to a small boat that appeared to be hooked to the *Adventure*. That, Josiah learned, was the longboat that carried crew and passengers to the shore when the ships were moored out in the harbor. Walls were called bulkheads, not walls, and the quarterdeck was where the captain and his crew stood to direct the ship. Josiah tried to memorize the heavy wooden wheel and the shiny instruments, but all too soon, he and Phillip English hurried off to a ladder that led below.

Suddenly it was dark, and the air smelled of a strange

mixture of horses and sugar. Josiah put his hand over his nose. He heard a squeak near his toe, and he thought something skittered over his boot. It felt like one of the rats that occasionally set up housekeeping in the Hutchinson barn. This was the cargo hold, not his favorite part of the ship.

It didn't appear to be Phillip English's, either. The longer he looked around, the deeper his scowl became. When his foot sloshed in water, the scowl broke into a stream of angry words. Simon entered the hold then and Mr. English turned on him.

"What's this, here?" he demanded.

"One of the men told me they began takin' on water on the way back, sir."

"Why wasn't the captain told?"

"He was, sir."

"I want to see him at once!"

"He's gone ashore, sir," Simon said.

"I did not ask where he was, Mister. I said I want to see him!"

"Aye, sir!"

Josiah had never thought he'd see Simon do anything at anyone else's command, but he was out of the hold, and probably off the ship, before Josiah could take another breath.

"Here's a ship that won't be sailing for a time," Phillip English muttered. Then he shook his head and led the way topside.

It wasn't long before a portly man rushed up the gangplank, clothes flying behind him as if he'd just climbed out of bed.

And it wasn't long before he retreated down the gang-plank, no longer the captain of the *Adventure*.

Mr. English and the blue-coated sailor then carried on a hurried conversation that Josiah could hear only snatches of. He gathered that the captain was relieved of his duties, and this first mate would be in charge of seeing that the necessary repairs were done on the *Adventure* while Mr. English searched for a new commander. Every voice was silent as Phillip English stomped off the ship, Josiah scurrying behind him. There was still so much he wanted to see, but this was not the time to ask for a longer tour.

Josiah was awakened early the next morning by a familiar voice shouting from the street. He stumbled to the window and peered through the gray mist to see Joseph Putnam grinning up at him.

"What? Not up and dressed?"

"It's—it's barely light!" Josiah said.

"Ah—it's a farm boy no longer, eh?" Joseph flashed a smile. "We'd best get on with those lessons, then, if you're to be a gentleman!"

Josiah threw on his clothes and tore down the steps. Joseph was already in the kitchen, munching on a macaroon and talking easily to Cook. Josiah watched him in admiration. If Joseph Putnam were his teacher, perhaps he could become like him.

But ten minutes into the first morning's lessons, Josiah was convinced that wouldn't happen, even if St. Peter himself were sent down to transform him.

They went into what Josiah would have called a best room, although the Englishes had several of these elegant sitting rooms in their mansion. As Joseph chatted about the villagers and his gallop down Ipswich Road this morning to avoid robbers, he spread his tools out on the table—ink, a copybook, and a book that Josiah recognized with a silent groan as *WINGATE'S ARITHMETIC*. He'd never gotten past the first page with Goodwife Porter.

The groan became louder when Joseph Putnam produced a hornbook. He had worn one around his neck at age six at the Porters'. It was a thin piece of wood, five inches long and two inches wide, with a piece of paper attached to its front. The paper, which was hard to come by in New England, was protected by a thin strip of clear horn, and held in place by a narrow leather strip and tiny nails. Across the top were printed the alphabet in large and small letters, some simple syllables, and the Lord's Prayer. At the two upper corners were crosses. At the lower end was a little handle pierced with a hole so it could be carried by a string, or placed around a schoolboy's neck.

The very sight of it made Josiah break out into droplets of sweat along his upper lip. He could never learn from these things before. Why should it be any different now? Already feeling the sag of failure, he slumped into a chair at the table.

Joseph Putnam's eyebrows shot up. "Something amiss, Josiah?"

Just that I'm dumb, Josiah thought. But he only shook his head.

"I'm of a mind to review first, just to see what already lurks in that head of yours, eh? Then we can proceed." He pushed the hornbook gently across the table. "Read off that alphabet for me, eh?"

Josiah struggled to focus on the letters that danced and teased from the top of the hornbook. He was able to do this once—barely—but that was a long time ago now, and even then it was like pulling teeth from a cat. With lips that moved like mud, he began to recite. His mind floundered. He rubbed the back of his neck. He blinked his eyes rapidly—the letters might make more sense if only he could look at them the right way. With a heavy sigh, he finally reached Z.

Josiah dared not look up. He didn't want to see the disappointment in Joseph Putnam's eyes.

"Good, then," young Putnam said briskly. "On to the Lord's Prayer, eh?"

Josiah didn't even have to look at this one. He'd known the prayer since he was four. He hadn't talked much until then, but it was one of the first things Hope taught him to say. The words flew from his lips.

When he was finished, Joseph quietly put the hornbook away and said nothing. When Josiah looked up cautiously, Joseph's forefingers were resting under his chin like a pair of pistols, while his clear eyes studied his student carefully.

"Did you go aboard Phillip's ship yesterday?" Joseph asked.

Josiah's eyes widened. "Aye—"

"And what did you learn there?"

"Learn?"

"Aye. What do you know now that you didn't know before yesterday?"

Josiah was confused, and he spoke slowly at first. "The big ship, the one that's being built now, is called a galleon." He looked at Joseph, who nodded.

"Go on, then," Joseph said.

"But the *Adventure*—she's the ship that just came back from her first voyage, y'see—that's a ketch. She's smaller and—and—has only two masts and a tiny forecastle and quarterdeck—though she's just what Mr. English needs for carrying goods to the West Indies."

Josiah's thoughts picked up speed, and with them his words. When he stopped to catch his breath, Joseph Putnam's smile was shining across the table.

"You learned all that in one morning?" he said.

"Aye—but there's more, sir—"

"And just how did you learn all this?"

Josiah looked at him blankly. "I—don't—I don't know—it was told to me, I suppose. And I saw it all—so I knew—"

Josiah's voice faded as he watched Joseph's face glow at him.

"What—what is it?" Josiah said.

"I was aboard ships in Boston harbor perhaps 20 times. I've even sailed up the rivers to Maine with my father. And I don't know any of that."

Josiah wasn't sure what that meant, and he frowned down at the tabletop. When he spoke again, Joseph's voice was soft.

"Do you want to be a seaman, Josiah?"

Josiah shrugged.

"Come on, man! It's etched in your face when you talk about it! A seaman is a fine, proud thing to be!"

"Aye," Josiah said. "I want to be—not a merchant like

Phillip English, but a sailor, a captain. I would never let a ship fall to ruin the way that captain did the *Adventure* after only one voyage!"

"Ah—it's a captain you want to be, then."

Josiah sunk his chin onto his chest. "I know I can never be that."

Once again, Joseph Putnam's eyebrows sprang up. "And why not, may I ask?"

Josiah stared at his hands. "Because—because—I'm not—because I'm dumb."

"Oh, I see! It was a dumb boy, then, who just recited the Lord's Prayer with every syllable perfect, eh? And was it that same 'dumb boy' who also rattled off more seaman's vocabulary than most of Hollingsworth's crew knows—after one hour aboard a vessel? The very same dumb boy who knows Indian cures—and heaven knows what else."

"But—but those—those are just things I learn myself. I can't learn in school!"

"Nay! You have not yet learned in school because everything so far has been words on a page." He pounded his finger on the hornbook and then, to Josiah's surprise, tossed it over his shoulder. It landed with a quiet thump on the wood floor. "You must learn to read if you're to be a ship's captain. But there are more ways to learn to read than plantin' you in front of some primer and waitin' for the words to come out of your mouth."

"Do you—do you know—those ways?" Josiah asked timidly.

"Not at this moment," Joseph Putnam admitted. "But I'm sure together we shall find them, eh, Captain?"

A light tapping came at the door, and Mary English slid her head in.

"And how are the lessons coming along?"

Josiah stared guiltily at the tabletop, but Joseph Putnam stood up and smiled at her. "Splendid!"

"Is he a promising student, then?"

"Aye!" Putnam sang out. "Would you like for him to show you?"

"Oh, please!"

Josiah's head jerked up, and his eyes grabbed wildly at his teacher. But Joseph Putnam ushered Mary English to a chair and scooped up the hornbook. Placing it in front of Josiah, he said, "Read the Lord's Prayer for Mrs. English."

Josiah looked up at him. Young Putnam's grin cut his face like a slice of apple. Josiah grinned back—and he began to "read."

✠ ⬥ ✠

Chapter Nine

oseph Putnam went off after dinner at noon, telling
Josiah to occupy himself while he found new "tools"
for their "adventure." Josiah still wasn't sure anything
could help him make sense of those loops and curls on a
piece of paper, but Joseph swung confidently down the street
as if finding the answer was only a matter of looking.

The house was quiet. Mr. English was off about his business, and Mary English and the babies were sleeping in the
heat of the afternoon. Josiah thought of Hope and his mother,
who were probably weeding the flax field in the scorching sun
or making candles in a steaming kitchen. One of those pangs
of longing clutched at his stomach. Determined to shake it
off, Josiah went out for a walk.

With minds of their own, his feet took him east down
Essex Street, but he stopped short before he reached
Shallop's Cove. A tiny sign on a pole above a side road bore

a name Josiah recognized—"English." He struggled to make sense of the rest. He wasn't sure, but it seemed to read, "English's Lane."

He owns the whole of the street? Josiah thought.

If it were his host's own lane, surely it was all right if he walked down it, Josiah decided. So he crossed Essex Street and made his way down.

It was a curious little street. There were a few houses, and Josiah wondered if these were some of the 13 buildings Phillip English owned. They were small, but they all bore the same marks of richness as the mansion. At the end of the street he noticed that one of the houses was not a house at all, but a shop. Josiah went to the window and peered in.

He and his father had gone to many of the shops along Ipswich Road—the blacksmith's where they had the horses shod and the cordwainer's where they had their own shoes made. But Josiah had never seen a shop like this.

In the window was a large shelf, and on it the shopkeeper had set out his wares for display. Treasures gleamed at him— colorful tins and intricate wood carvings and gold—

Josiah took a sharp breath. Gold chains. In a flash of memory, Josiah saw another just like the ones in the window. Spilling from the collar of Ann Putnam.

He looked around uncertainly, and for a full minute he stood with his hand on the doorknob. When the door fell open to let out a customer, Josiah slipped inside.

The shop was cool and dark, and the air smelled of pleasant things Josiah didn't recognize. As his eyes grew used to the dim light, he saw that the walls were lined with shelves bearing more and bigger treasures than the ones in the window. A shriveled-looking old man sat behind a high desk in the corner of the room and peered over his crooked nose at Josiah.

"What d'ye want, boy?" he said.

"I—I simply—I—"

"Who are ye?"

"I'm—I'm—"

"Great Jehovah, boy! Out with it!" the old man cried.

"I'm Josiah Hutchinson!" he sputtered. "I'm a guest—a guest of Phillip English."

As if by magic, the old man's shriveled face smoothed, and he managed a smile that brought his nose down to his chin.

"Why didn't ye say so?" he said with a cackle. "What might I do for ye, then? Did Mr. English send ye?"

"No!" He wanted to add, *And please don't tell him I was here!* but the old man bustled from his stool and took Josiah's arm.

"Ye just look about all ye like," he said. "We've some fine treasures here, fine treasures. Mr. English brings them from the West Indies—we've teas and spices and gold pieces the likes of which ye've never seen."

"These all—all belong to Mr. English?" Josiah said. "The gold chains as—as well?"

"Aye. Buys them in the Indies, he does, and brings them here to sell. What isn't carried off by thieves, that is."

"Thieves?"

"Aye! Come right into the shop at times, they do, and sneak off with the goods." His crinkled face cracked into a smile again. "I have to be sure I know everyone who comes in. That's why I questioned ye so close."

Josiah moved his mouth carefully as he asked his next question. "Have you—have you ever had one of the—the gold chains stolen?"

The old man scowled fiercely as he moved to the shelf where the necklaces rippled across the wood. "Aye. Thieves love these, they do. See how easy they slip into a pocket?"

With a twist of his wiry old wrist, the shopkeeper poked the end of a gold chain into the pouch Josiah had tied to his britches. It slithered into the opening and disappeared inside.

"Simple as that." The old man shook his head. "I don't even see they're gone for a while—and the thieves are probably halfway out to sea by then."

He held out a bony hand, and Josiah quickly fumbled open the pouch and pulled out the chain. It was the first time he had ever held anything made of gold, and the metal felt smooth and cool against his palm.

"You like, eh?" said the old man.

Josiah shrugged. It was strictly against Puritan law to even have an interest in gold. But he knew at least one Puritan who did.

The old man was ready to chat now and probably would have for the rest of the afternoon, but Josiah finally managed to leave by promising to come back another day. His mind was spinning as he ran across a wide, rocky field toward the harbor. How had Ann Putnam gotten hold of one of Phillip English's gold chains? It was the only place except Boston where such a thing would have come from. And the old man said thieves stole them all the time. Thieves? Was Ann herself a thief? Josiah shook his head. That was foolish—impossible, even. But she was wearing it secretly so maybe she'd gotten it from a thief. One of the Putnams—a cousin or brother? Was it the same thief who'd tried to rob Josiah and Joseph Putnam on the Ipswich Road? That thief had himself worn a ring—a ring with an S on it.

Josiah reached the harbor and walked along the road that ran beside it. Something that started with a D, another sign on a pole told him. It might actually be worth it to learn to read, he decided.

He was headed now toward Phillip English's wharf, and his steps slowed as he drew nearer. Mr. English had not said he couldn't visit the wharf, but he hadn't made it clear that he could, either. Still, it couldn't hurt to just walk around, as long as he didn't get in anyone's way.

He was sure he'd made the right choice when he reached the new galleon, and Juan smiled and bobbed his black head. *If it weren't right for me to be here, he would run me off,* Josiah thought.

Juan went straight back to work, and Josiah gazed at the almost-ship. It was hard to believe that just a few months ago, the wood that formed the galleon's sleek lines had been trees standing in Salem Village woods—and then piles of timber in the Porter/Hutchinson sawmill. He felt his chin tilt proudly. In a way, this ship did belong to him.

Juan didn't look up as Josiah wandered down the Point of Rocks. In fact, no one seemed to notice him at all. The wharf was alive with activity as sailors dashed about, unloading lumpy bags from yet another ship that had come in. It was a ketch, Josiah observed, and then smiled to himself.

Something was definitely happening around the *Adventure,* and Josiah was drawn to the action on her dock at the end of the wharf. Her decks were crawling with seamen on their knees, scrubbing with wiry-looking brushes out of buckets sloshing with soap, or on ladders slapping thick, shiny paint over her bulkheads. There was so much more he wanted to know about what they were doing, what secrets lay within the ship's belly that he hadn't yet seen. With the trouble of repairing the ship and finding a new captain, it was sure Philip English had time for no more tours. Would it hurt—

Before he had even considered it carefully, Josiah's feet were crossing the gangplank. No one even looked at him twice, much less asked him what he was about there. *Then it must be all right,* he kept assuring himself. Only the blue-coated first mate was at the top of the gangplank, his back turned as he talked to a scrubbing seaman on the forecastle deck. Josiah tried to convince himself that he would have spoken to the sailor if he'd noticed him, that he wasn't really sneaking as he slipped past him and took the nearest ladder below.

His first stop would be the cargo hold, where the real work was being done. If he wasn't supposed to be there, surely he would be asked to leave—if they saw him.

He remembered the way to the hold, but he didn't remember it being so dark. With the hatch closed behind him, he couldn't see his hands as he stretched them out in front of him. He reached for the damp bulkhead and felt his way along toward where Phillip English had discovered the water at his feet.

He was surprised no one was working down here. He'd wanted to be alone to explore, but now—it was spooky. He considered turning back, but this might be his only chance to touch and see the ship's inside magic.

It was obvious no one had spent any time down here as yet. The air was still rank with the odor of horses, and Josiah tripped over bits of debris as he went along. Hadn't Mr. English told Simon to clean up the hold after it was unloaded?

Josiah's heart sped up. He'd forgotten that Simon worked for Mr. English. But he straightened his shoulders bravely. Simon didn't go to sea with the ships, so perhaps he wouldn't be aboard the *Adventure*. He was probably busy unloading that other ketch that had just come into port.

Just then his foot splashed into a puddle of water. Josiah crouched down to examine the bulkhead above it with his fingers. Had Mr. English discovered a leak here?

He didn't find a hole, but his hands did come to a heavy hook attached to the bulkhead. It must be for fastening ropes to hold the cargo in place, he decided.

His eyes were used to the light now, and he searched the floor for something the rope would attach to there.

"Ah!" he said out loud when he found it. It was a wheel with a grooved rim, and rope could be pulled through to hold it tight. Curious, Josiah put the toe of his boot on it and gave it a push. He was instantly on the deck, his backside stinging.

He pulled back on his foot, but it didn't move. Josiah

pushed himself up with his arms and saw two things at the same time. His boot toe was stuck between the grooves—and a large rat was headed straight toward him.

✠ ⊷ ✠

osiah choked back a scream as he tugged in a panic at his foot. With every yank, the wheel turned a little more and pinched his toe a little tighter. He looked around wildly for the rat.

It had stopped a few skitter-steps from him and was on its hind legs, sizing him up. It was bigger than any of the rodents Josiah had chased around his father's barn, and its sharp yellow teeth sent shivers through him.

"Get back!" he shouted. "Go on, then!"

The rat went down on all fours and crouched. Josiah's mind raced, and he felt around for something to throw at it or push it back with. His hand fell on his pouch and with fumbling fingers he untied it and swung it at the rat.

It retreated several steps and stopped, sniffing the air and fiddling with its fingers.

"Get back now!" Josiah shouted again, and he swung the

pouch as hard as he could. It flew out of his hand over the rat's head. The animal rushed toward him at a gallop.

"No!" Josiah screamed.

Suddenly he was blinded by light as the hatch door flew open. He didn't dare take his eyes off the rat whose silhouette was now poised at his knee. Then Josiah gasped as he saw a hand grab its tail, lift it off the deck, and dangle it inches from his nose.

"No!" he screamed again.

"I suppose I'd be cryin' 'no!' too, farm boy, if I'd gotten myself in this kind of fix," a familiar voice hissed in his ear.

Josiah closed his eyes. He didn't know which was worse, being bitten by a rat or rescued by Simon.

"Well, well, then." Simon rocked down to his knees and swung the rat a little farther from Josiah's face. The animal was squealing and squirming, and Josiah felt like doing the same thing.

Instead he said quietly, "Would you—could you—please—unloose my foot, eh?"

"Oh, but surely!" Simon cried. Josiah groaned silently. Simon's voice was singing with pure glee. He wasn't going to get off easily.

"But first," he went on, "I think you owe me an explanation, do you not?"

"For—for what?" Josiah watched the rat, which Simon was now bouncing over his head.

"For why you would be down here in the hold of the *Adventure*. It's my hold, you know."

Josiah wanted to scream out, *It isn't*. But he bit his tongue.

"Now, the mighty Mr. English did tell me to clean it up a

bit—so I suppose this is as good a place as any to start. You're a pretty large piece of garbage, Master Hutchinson."

Josiah stayed still and watched the rat, still swinging like a pendulum over his head.

"So—answer my question," Simon said.

"I—I wanted to see—y'know—the damage."

"Ah, and did Mr. English himself send you as ship's inspector?"

Josiah considered lying. Simon dropped the rat in front of his eyes, and Josiah quickly shook his head. Simon gave a high-pitched giggle that would put Sarah Proctor to shame.

"So the high and mighty Mr. English doesn't know his little guest has snuck aboard his vessel to spy."

"I—I wasn't spying—I was merely—I'm interested."

Simon pulled the rat back and stuck his face close to Josiah's. "It matters not *why* you are here but *that* you are here without his highness's permission. Do you know what kind of trouble you'll get into for this, farm boy?"

Slowly, he shook his head. Josiah didn't know what kind— he just knew that trouble alone meant he'd go back to Salem Village in shame.

Simon sat cross-legged on the deck facing him and swung the rat above his own head by the tail. Josiah was starting to feel sorry for it. It was screeching and clawing the air in terror.

"Suppose we were to strike a bargain, you and I?" Simon said. "Suppose I were to turn you loose from that sheave there and toss this rat out a porthole and suppose you in turn were to pay me to keep my mouth shut about your being here?"

"I can't pay you!" Josiah cried. "I—I—I have no money of my own."

"I—I—I wasn't talking about money."

Simon's voice mocked him, and Josiah's cheeks burned. He gave his foot a violent tug, but it only caught tighter. Simon swung the rat playfully back and forth in front of him.

"I was talking," Simon said, "about a different sort of payment, which you can very easily provide."

Josiah's skin crawled with disgust. It might be better to take his punishment and go home in disgrace than do anything for this boy who was no better than a rat himself.

"They say that the cook at Mr. English's house is famous for her rare treats. Am I correct?"

Josiah nodded sullenly.

"Pies and pastries the likes of which an orphan boy like myself can only dream of."

Good, Josiah thought.

Simon brought his face so close to Josiah's that his spiky red hair touched Josiah's sweaty curls. "I will let you go on the promise that tomorrow you will bring me a sampling of the delicate treasures from Mr. English's cupboard." He grinned smugly. "And if you do not return with them, I shall inform Mr. English of your presence here today."

Josiah stared into the boy's narrow colorless eyes for a long time. It would be easy to do. He was welcome to the contents of the cupboard anytime. But to steal from his host, the very person who was providing his education, and to meet the demands of a scoundrel like this—

But if he didn't, he'd see the disappointment in everyone's eyes—Mama, Papa, Hope, Mr. English, Joseph Putnam—just because he'd been foolish enough to slip aboard the *Adventure* without permission. Not to study with young Joseph. Not to be able to read and learn his numbers so he could become a captain—and give slimy characters like Simon orders—

"Good then!" Josiah blurted out. "I shall be back tomorrow —after dinner."

Simon leaned back and looked at him carefully. Then slowly he got up and pitched the rat through the hatch. Josiah heard it land with a thud and a squeal. The tall redhead laughed scornfully as he pushed the wheel back the other way and freed Josiah's foot.

"You could have loosed it yourself all along," Simon said. "But it takes years of work to learn those things. Don't be fancyin' yourself a sailor, farm boy."

Josiah scrambled up to go, but Simon clawed his shoulder and pulled him back down. With his face close to Josiah's again, Simon said, "Come after supper, in the evening. I have the anchor watch then. We can have a bit of a chat, eh, while I dine?"

"I'll bring you food." Josiah felt his cheeks blaze with anger. "But I don't have to—I shan't—there'll be no 'chatting' with you!"

Simon wiggled his eyebrows. "We shall see." And with a shove he let Josiah go.

The afternoon wind had begun to gust through the harbor, kicking up whitecaps in the shallower waters and bringing a haze into the air. But Josiah's face was still hot with anger as he bolted down the gangplank and tore down the wharf. He hated Simon, and he wanted to get far away from him as fast as he could.

But he also hated himself right now, and there was no

getting away from that. He excused himself from the table after picking at his supper and spent the rest of the evening in his room, staring from the window out at the hazy harbor. Would there never be a time when he was not in trouble, not under the thumb of someone more powerful than he, not in terror of what would happen next?

So many people had told him—Papa, the Widow Hooker, even the Reverend Higginson in his sermons—to go to God when he was in trouble. But right now, Josiah couldn't. God must be sick of him by now, making the same mistakes over and over like he did. He would have to get out of this one by himself. And he was sure no amount of schooling would help.

He tossed and turned all night. When he did finally fall asleep, he dreamed he was aboard a galleon whose captain was a giant rat with red hair. He himself scrubbed the hold with a brush while the rat-captain dangled above him from a rope tied to the sheave.

So he was puffy-faced and grumpy when he arrived in the schoolroom for his second day's lessons. Young Joseph Putnam, on the other hand, was shiny-eyed, and he rubbed his hands together as if he were about to sit down to a Thanksgiving feast. When Josiah was seated at the table across from him, Joseph reached into his jacket and pulled out a slim dark green volume with gold lettering.

"Do you know what this is, Captain?" His eyes twinkled.

"No," Josiah said glumly. "I can't read, remember?"

Joseph ignored him. "This is a book by Sir Henry Manwayring."

"Who?"

"A master of your favorite subject—the sea. This is the finest text of instruction in seamanship there is, and you, Josiah Hutchinson—*Captain* Josiah Hutchinson—are going to learn to read it. Go on, then, have a look at it."

In spite of the shadows that lurked in the corners of his mind, Josiah took the book in his hands, and his thoughts began to brighten. The usual tangle of words and letters made Josiah's eyes burn, but there were also pictures, with words beside them. Almost immediately, Josiah's eyes fell on a pencil drawing of something familiar. He put his finger on the word next to it and felt the letters in his mouth. Yes, they matched.

He looked up at Joseph. "Sheave."

Joseph Putnam could deliver smiles that paled the stars, but the one that spread across his handsome face now out-dazzled them all. It was a smile Josiah wanted to bring to that face again and again. Maybe that would make him not such a bad person, after all.

Joseph Putnam reached into his bag and pulled out more of what he called "tools." There was the arithmetic book—which he assured Josiah was merely there so he could learn to find his latitude with a cross staff. There was a Bible—because a man would get nowhere in his chosen trade without a knowledge of the Lord. And there was a set of wooden blocks, with raised letters of the alphabet carved out of their sides. Josiah immediately picked these up and ran his fingers over the letters. The A came to life at his touch. It was different, feeling it rather than just looking at it.

"Aye, then, Captain," young Putnam said, "shall we begin?"

The morning passed in a flash as Josiah arranged and rearranged the letters and discovered words like port and fore and aft, which Joseph found in Sir Henry's book. He would have plenty to show William and Ezekiel—and Simon. Only once or twice did thoughts of tonight's errand cloud his mind. And only once or twice did he find his hands sweating and rubbing the back of his neck.

After noon dinner, Josiah was allowed to sit back while Joseph Putnam read to him. He'd always loved being read to. His father read to the family from the Bible every night. Joseph read almost as well as Papa—but it was what he read that fascinated Josiah.

It was the story of a prophet named Jonah whom God instructed to go to a city called Nineveh to warn the people that He was upset with them for their sinfulness. But Jonah was afraid to do it, so he tried to run away from God by boarding a ship and going out to sea.

Josiah leaned forward with interest and watched Joseph's mouth carefully as he read.

While Jonah was at sea, a terrible storm came up, and none of the sailors could do anything to save the ship. If the storm kept on, the ship would be wrecked and they would all drown. Jonah knew it was his fault that the storm raged, because God was angry with him for trying to hide, so he told the sailors to throw him overboard, which they did. In the meantime, the storm was calmed and the ship was safe. God arranged for a large fish to swallow Jonah, and he stayed in the fish's belly for three nights. While he was there, Jonah had time to think, and he realized he needed to follow God's orders. So he prayed to God, who had the fish spit him out. He went safely ashore and on to the city of Nineveh.

"I thought you might like a story about the sea," Joseph Putnam said as he quietly closed the Bible. "There are plenty more. Soon you can read them for yourself."

But Josiah wasn't thinking about the ship or the sea in the story. He was thinking about Jonah trying to hide from God. For a fleeting moment, he thought he might tell Joseph Putnam about his bargain with Simon and his fear of going to God with the story. But as quickly as the idea came to him, he brushed it away. Joseph was becoming so proud of him. He didn't want to disappoint him now.

As the afternoon wore on into evening, Josiah became more and more restless. Once again his stomach churned at the supper table and he could barely eat a bite, even though Cook made a codfish stew that was thick and rich and full of good-smelling spices. His eyes grew wide when she put a plate of macaroons on the table, though. Perhaps he could slip a few into his pouch now, so he wouldn't have to sneak into the kitchen to steal them later. But even before his hand reached his hip, he remembered the pouch was still in the hold of the *Adventure*, where he'd thrown it at the rat.

"Is there something troubling you, Josiah?" Mary English asked kindly.

"For a boy who has spent his whole day bent over his books, you don't have much of an appetite," Mr. English put in.

Joseph Putnam just looked at him carefully.

"Nay," Josiah said. "Nay—I'm just—I'm not hungered yet."

"Well, should you become hungered in the night, you just slip down to the kitchen and have yourself a feast," Mary English said. "Cook has shown you where she keeps things, I hope?"

Josiah nodded. The guilt, he was sure, was printed on his face like words in those books in the schoolroom.

Phillip English laughed. "Joseph! It looks as if you need to work the boy harder, eh? Now, then—I have a question for all of you."

Josiah tried to pay attention.

"Has anyone spied my boatswain's pipe about? It seems to have sprouted legs of its own and taken off."

"That beauty of a pipe of yours is gone?" Joseph said.

"Aye—I know I had it on yesterday when Josiah and I were aboard the *Adventure*. Perhaps I took it off while we were looking about. Well, it was nowhere to be found when I had a mind to put it on this morning. It will turn up, I suspect."

Still, his face was grim for a minute. *He thinks someone has stolen it,* Josiah thought. But he had other things to think about.

It seemed as if supper would never be over. Mrs. English finally went upstairs with the baby girls, and Mr. English and Joseph retired to Mr. English's study on the second floor, and Cook put the last of the pots to rest and went off to her own quarters. It was just before sunset, and Josiah's heart was racing. The small bit of supper he had eaten threatened to bubble up from his stomach.

He lingered in the yard for a while until the house was still. Then stepping carefully, he made his way through the back

door and into the big kitchen. *Cook said to help myself —
and so did Mrs. English,* one of Josiah's voices told him. But
another answered, *Yes, but they meant for you. You're
stealing if you take it for Simon, and you know it!*

He shook off both voices and quietly pulled open the
cupboard door. There it all was, plate after pewter plate of
apple pie, spice cake, candied fruit, freshly baked bread, and
his beloved macaroons. Josiah sighed anxiously. He would
probably never be able to enjoy them again.

He looked around for something to wrap things in. The
linen napkins were on a shelf on the other side of the room.
He dove for them and had just grabbed one when he heard
voices in the hall. Dropping the napkin, he darted around the
room like a trapped rabbit. Just as the voices began to filter
under the kitchen door, he threw open the large cabinet that
held the dishes, squeezed under the bottom shelf, and pulled
the door closed after him. Through the crack he saw the
kitchen door swing open and the elegant skirts of Mary
English swish into the room.

Ruth came in behind her. Mrs. English was laughing her
clear tinkling laugh.

"It matters not how much men eat for their supper, Ruth,"
she said. "They must still have their delicacies in the study an
hour later!"

"Aye," said Ruth.

Through the crack Josiah watched in anguish as Mrs.
English moved toward the pie cabinet and stopped short as
she saw its doors flung wide open.

"Cook must have been in a hurry tonight," she said.

"Aye," Ruth said. "She even left a napkin on the floor. Shall I fetch one of the pewter plates?"

Josiah's heart stopped, and he tried to make himself disappear into the bottom of the dish cabinet.

"Nay. Let us use that lovely tray there atop the breakfront, since we've our special guest Mr. Putnam with us this evening."

Josiah could hardly keep from exploding with relief. He put both shaking hands over his mouth.

"Mr. Putnam is a handsome one, is he not?" Mrs. English chatted on.

"Aye!"

"It's no wonder he's to be married this October next."

"Married! So young?"

"Aye. He's but 20 years. His wife is but 16."

"Sixteen!"

For an awful moment, Josiah was sure he had been the one to blurt that out. But his trembling hands were still planted firmly over his mouth. It was Ruth who was staring at Mrs. English, the words still dancing on her lips.

"Aye, but there are special reasons for making this match so early on. The girl, you see, is a Porter. Constance is her name, and a beauty she is."

Constance, Josiah's thoughts nearly screamed. *Joseph Putnam was marrying Constance Porter?*

"You see, Joseph Putnam will inherit his father's fortune when he marries, and since he is the only son of Martha Putnam, he will inherit her wealth as well when she dies. That will give him considerable power, power they need in Salem

Village, as far as I can tell. Phillip says the match won't hurt the Porters any, either. With the Porters and Joseph Putnam teamed together, there is nothing they won't be able to do in Salem Village. Will you serve these to the men, Ruth? I must be back upstairs with the children."

"Aye."

"Oh—and Ruth—if you see Mr. English's boatswain's pipe about, will you tell him?"

"Aye."

Josiah hardly noticed that they both left the kitchen. He sat for a long time in the bottom of the dish cupboard. When Hope and the other girls giggled about marriage, they made it sound like something you did because you wanted to. Even though Josiah couldn't see the sense in it, they seemed to think it was something delicious to look forward to.

Mary English had made it sound like some trap Joseph Putnam and poor young Constance Porter were being lured into. Josiah had long felt that in spite of his father's love for old Israel Porter, the Porters were a sneaky lot. Thinking about it always left him feeling a little empty inside.

But suddenly he snapped back to the present and climbed carefully out of the cupboard. The sun was almost gone from the kitchen as he stuffed several pieces of spice cake and a half loaf of bread into napkins and tucked them under his arms. He was grateful for the gathering darkness as he slipped out of the kitchen.

✛ ✛ ✛

Chapter Eleven

The wharf was a different place at night. Everything was quiet except for the splashing of the surf against the pilings and the blowing of the wind high overhead. No one was around, and Josiah felt more alone than he'd ever felt. Even Juan wasn't there to nod and nod until Josiah was sure it was all right to be there.

He knew it wasn't all right to be there, and the steps that hurried him toward the *Adventure* were guilty ones. Twice he almost tossed the cake and bread into the sea and ran back to Joseph Putnam. But the picture of disappointment in everyone's eyes drove him right to the bottom of the gangplank.

He was halfway up when a familiar voice rasped out, "Who goes there?"

Josiah barely managed to say, "Aye!" when Simon was down the plank with a lantern in his hand, pulling Josiah on board the ship. He held him tightly by the arm, and Josiah

almost cried out in pain. The bruises from the last time someone had grabbed him there weren't completely healed yet.

Simon dragged him on and finally shoved him against the
bulkhead several feet aft of the gangplank.

"We'll sit here," Simon said. "I have the anchor watch
tonight. I have to guard the ship against—" he wiggled his
eyebrows wickedly "—*thieves,* while the rest of the crew
sleeps."

That sounded like a brave job to Josiah. He'd have given
up more than macaroons to do it. But Simon obviously found
it beneath him, and he screwed his face up against the idea as
if it reeked of some horrible odor.

"So, what have you brought me, farm boy?"

Without a word, Josiah plunked the two bundles into
Simon's lap and got up to leave. But Simon yanked him down
by the pant leg, nearly pulling his britches off in the process.

"I hate to eat all alone," he said into Josiah's face. His eyes
glimmered as he opened the first napkin and crammed a
whole piece of spice cake into his mouth. That didn't stop
him from talking, and Josiah looked away as crumbs and half-
chewed food spewed out with his words.

"I'll be goin' out on the next voyage," Simon said.

As if I cared, Josiah thought.

"Started out as a cut tail, I did. Do you know what that is,
farm boy?"

Josiah shrugged.

"I worked aboard a fishing boat before I was even your
age . . ."

As if you're so much older now.

" . . . to learn the 'art and mystery of fishing.' I had to cut a wedge from the tail of every fish I caught so at the end of the trip they knew how much my share of the profit was." He gave a short, hard laugh. "I caught so many I was runnin' them right out of business, so they traded me off to Mr. English. Mr. English is part of the 'Codfish Aristocracy' y'see. Made his start by shippin' codfish. Thinks he's high and mighty now because he trades in molasses and gold. He thinks he's the richest man in Salem Town, and well he may be—but not for long if he doesn't start tradin' slaves the way Mr. Hollingsworth plans to. English already treats us like slaves— why doesn't he make some money from it, eh? He thinks I'm no better than a common boy who loads and unloads his cargo and cleans his holds, but I'll be aboard the next voyage. I'll show them all then, eh?"

You'll show them you're a lazy scoundrel, Josiah thought.

Simon picked the last crumbs from the bread, and Josiah stood up, this time jumping out of Simon's reach.

"You'll be staying until the end of my watch," Simon said, as if there would be no arguing with that. "Eight bells. Eight little bells will ring, and we'll know the watch is over—"

"If I stay gone that long I'll be caught and—and—and sent back, and I will have nothing to lose by telling—about you— you'll never go on a voyage!"

Josiah hadn't known he was going to say that. He'd just known he was angry. "I'm going now," he said.

"But you'll be back tomorrow night."

"No!"

"Then I shall have to betray our little secret."

Their eyes locked in the darkness. Josiah could stand to look at him no longer, and he turned on his heel and headed for the gangplank.

"Tomorrow night, farm boy—or you shall be exposed!"

And so a routine began. Josiah studied with Joseph Putnam in the mornings and was read to in the afternoons. At dinner and supper he managed to slip slices of bread and pieces of dried fruit into his shirt and used the same napkins over and over to carry them, so he wouldn't have to risk being caught in the kitchen. In the evenings when the adults were settled in, he hurried through the darkness down English's Lane, down Derby Street—as he learned that word that started with a D was—and down the wharf.

When he had the anchor watch, Simon would wait for him at tne top of the gangplank. When he didn't, he would distract the attention of the crewman who did, and silently order Josiah to slip past him and meet him in the shadows. On those evenings, Simon would take him below the forecastle deck where the crew slept. Usually there were six seamen aboard the *Adventure*, but when it was in the harbor, most of them went home to their families at night, and Simon and a few other cargo men slept in their quarters. Josiah learned from Sir Henry's book that they would hurry back to the ship any time they saw the blue flag with the white rectangle in the center flying from the signal mast. That was the Blue Peter, which meant "come now."

There was never anyone else in the crew's quarters when Simon pushed Josiah inside. Josiah didn't see how anyone else could fit in there, anyway. The cabin was small and cramped and dark, and Simon had only a lumpy cot that hung on the wall. It had a kind of mattress on it, and sometimes Josiah saw him stuff his few leftover chunks of food under it for safekeeping.

My father's cows live better than this, Josiah thought the first time he looked around the quarters. *And we would feed those crumbs to the pigs.*

One night, as he watched Simon slump in a dark corner and gobble down dried fruit tarts as if he hadn't eaten in a year, Josiah felt a pang. It was damp and dingy in the cabin, and Simon looked thin and desperate, devouring the food like a lonely animal.

When Simon looked at him, though, his faded-out eyes were suspicious. "What are you lookin' at, farm boy?"

Josiah shrugged.

Simon sniffed and stood up to scratch, then turned his back and lifted the mattress. But he didn't slide any tidbits of food under it. He seemed more concerned with being sure something that was already there was safely in its place. A shiver went through Josiah. He was sure he'd seen the gleam of gold and jewels there under the mattress. When Simon stood up, Josiah quickly turned his head away before Simon saw him watching. What might he have hidden under that mattress? Something gold? A boatswain's pipe, perhaps?

"Come on, farm boy." Simon batted him lightly on the side of the head. "It's time you were gone." He laughed harshly. "But I think you were already gone—wherever it is you go when you float away like that."

Six weeks flew by that way. Going to the wharf with food hidden beneath his shirt became such a habit that after a while, Josiah almost forgot he was stealing to cover up his mistake. He even stopped worrying he would be seen. If Juan were still there, working on the galleon late in the evening, he scarcely looked up when Josiah went by, as much as Josiah would have liked to become friends. And there were never any sailors running around the wharf or fishermen bringing in their catch of cod and mackerel. The workday was over. The wharf was quiet. No one knew.

Sometimes it was only on Sundays when he saw his family at Meeting that the guilt bobbed to the surface. They were all so kind—Papa letting him sit beside his mother instead of in the boys' gallery to avoid the attacks of the other children, Mama bringing him a cloth bookmark she'd embroidered for him one night, Hope whispering that Ezekiel and William were lost without him, and that big, strong Giles Porter wasn't nearly so much a help to their father as Josiah was. It was a kindness that was hard to enjoy, because he knew if they discovered what he was up to, they would never trust him again. It was hard, he decided, to accept kindness you didn't deserve.

But on Monday mornings when Joseph Putnam returned from the village and they began their studies again, the guilty feelings settled back down to some quiet place inside him once more. He was learning fast, and Joseph praised him every day. "Aye, Captain!" he would cry when Josiah would compute a sum or read aloud from Sir Henry. "You'll be taking a ship to sea afore you're 20, you will!"

Josiah thought a few times that if he became smart enough, the discovery of his lying and stealing might not seem so terrible.

But he didn't really believe God would accept that reasoning. He still couldn't go to the window at night and pray. Why would God listen to someone who was doing wrong on purpose and couldn't stop?

He thought sometimes of asking Simon if his debt were paid yet and they could stop their secret meetings. He'd brought him pie and cakes for longer than most men spent in jail for their crimes. He was still afraid, though, when Simon looked down at him with his no-color eyes or grabbed him a little too roughly to move him here or there to keep out of the sight of someone in the shadows. If Simon could do something so evil as steal Mr. English's boatswain's pipe, what else might he do? And besides, he suspected that Simon, in his way, liked having him there.

That became clear one night when Simon had the anchor watch, and they stood together on the forecastle deck while Simon practically licked the napkin of crumbs. The air over the harbor was growing thick with fog, and Josiah was anxious to leave. As he started to reach for the napkin, he noticed that something strange had happened while they were standing there.

The wharf was almost completely smothered with a heavy blanket of fog. As Josiah looked at Simon, he could see nothing but Simon. Behind him, above him, below him, were all cloaked in mist. Simon looked as if he were trapped in a private world where nothing seemed quite real.

But as he watched him, Josiah noticed something else. From the waist of Simon's britches dangled Josiah's whistle pouch, bulging now with what looked like more than just his wooden whistle. Hope had spent hours sewing it for him, and now it hung on the body of this, this scoundrel!—holding heaven knew what. It was more than even Josiah could swallow.

But when he opened his mouth to protest, Simon turned to look at him.

"They're like scarves," he said.

Josiah stared. "What?"

"Those pieces of the mist that drift out there. They're like scarves." He hissed through his teeth. "Many's the night I wished I had a scarf—damp as it gets."

Then he shrugged as if he wanted to forget he'd even said it, to Josiah or himself or anyone else.

Josiah closed his mouth and held his hand out for the napkin.

"Good-bye," he said.

Simon stuffed the napkin into Josiah's palm. "See you tomorrow night?" It was the first time he had ever said it as a question. Josiah nodded, and then he ran. Someday he would get his pouch back—and perhaps even know what was in it. But tonight, Simon's eyes were soft and Josiah thought that for the moment, Simon needed the pouch more than he did.

In his last lesson with Joseph Putnam he had read aloud a whole paragraph from Sir Henry's book. It had told about the fog, and Josiah decided as he hurried through it that night that every word Sir Henry had said was true.

"The fog can play havoc with your judgment," the book

had said. Joseph Putnam explained that havoc was something like confusion—and Josiah was confused as soon as his feet hit the wharf.

Where was that little neck of land that led to Salem Town? It seemed that it was in that direction away from the sound of the water splashing against the docks' pilings. But as he stumbled away from it, it fell silent. He stopped to listen. Nothing. Had the sea disappeared entirely? Was he already back on the mainland? What if he'd turned the wrong way? Was he about to tumble over the Point of Rocks and into the water?

With his hands stretched out in front of him he crept on, even though he could no longer see his fingers. He screamed when they thudded against something hard and damp.

"Quíen está aquí?" a voice called out.

Josiah froze.

"Quíen está aquí?" the voice said again. Even in the fog Josiah knew it was closer now, but when the words shouted still again, into his ear, he jumped and screamed. Someone grabbed his arm, and out of the mist a face took shape close to his. It was Juan.

"Señor Hutchinson!" His raisin teeth appeared in a smile, and he began to bob his head in delight. Josiah wanted to dissolve into a puddle. He must be standing right next to the galleon. He wasn't far from the warehouse.

"I—I'm lost, Juan!"

Juan nodded happily and took him by the arm. Josiah was surprised at how gentle his touch was.

With sure steps, Juan led him through the mist, all the way past the warehouse and onto the mainland of Salem Town.

Gums gleaming in a grin, he pointed toward the galleon and backed toward it, waving.

Please don't tell anyone you saw me out here, Josiah wanted to call after him. But then he laughed out loud. Juan wouldn't tell anyone. He didn't speak English.

Josiah was too happy to be out of the heaviest of the fog and safely onto dry land to worry about being caught slipping in through the kitchen door. His heart was light as he ran up English's Lane, down Essex Street, and into the English kitchen. Right away he heard the voices from the study. One of them was his father's.

"He told no one where he was going?" Joseph Hutchinson said.

Josiah flattened himself against the wall and held his breath.

"We've not asked him to," Mr. English said. "He goes out every evening for a bit of a walk after supper—though I've never known him to be out this late."

He knows I go out! Josiah thought wildly. *Does he know where? Is he about to tell?*

"I'm a bit concerned about him being out in the fog, though," Mr. English said. "If he goes too near the wharf, it's a simple matter to become confused—"

"He had no business to worry you when he's a guest in your home," Papa said. "If he's not returned within the hour, Phillip—"

Before he could finish the sentence, Josiah peeled himself from the wall and tapped at the study door.

"Aye," said Mr. English.

Josiah slowly pushed open the door and stuck his head in. To his surprise, Joseph Putnam rushed to the doorway to meet him. He hadn't said a word, and Josiah hadn't even known he was in the room. "Josiah!" he cried. "I trust you had a pleasant walk—and we have an even more pleasant surprise for you!"

Josiah blinked for a moment. It was almost as if Joseph were protecting him.

"Josiah," Papa said.

He held out his hand, and Josiah slid under it. The hand came down on his shoulder but not harshly. Josiah reminded himself to breathe.

"Good evening, son."

"Papa."

There was an uneasy silence as his father searched his face. *What is he looking for,* Josiah thought. *Proof that I can be trusted? Proof that I am in no trouble? Proof that I will bring no shame on him? Proof that I think before I act?*

Josiah swallowed hard. So many times in the schoolroom these past weeks, he had had the urge to tell Joseph Putnam of the trap he was in. He had that same feeling now. Perhaps if he were honest, it could all be taken care of—

Joseph Putnam cleared his throat. "You are just in time, Josiah. We were about to share a cup of cider, and I thought some reading from you would round out the evening, eh?"

Papa's deep-set eyes seemed to spring forward. "Josiah—read to us?"

"Aye. Perhaps from Sir Henry, eh, Josiah?"

Josiah's mouth went dry as Joseph pulled the slim green volume from his jacket and held it out to him.

"Splendid!" Phillip English said. "Hutchinson, sit you here."

The men settled into their seats, and Josiah fumbled for the passage he had read that morning, about the fog. His fingers seemed to turn to stumps as he pawed for the page, and when at last he found it, the words swam before his eyes like so many fish in the harbor. He looked up at Joseph Putnam. His teacher said nothing, but his eyes were shining. He nodded, so slightly no one saw but Josiah. The words on his face said, "I have faith in you."

Gulping down the lump in his throat, Josiah looked at the page again and his mouth began to move. It was slow at first, but the words were clear. "Fog," he began, "can play havoc with your judgment."

It seemed as if he himself were enclosed in fog, the way Simon had been on the deck. There was no sound around him, no one else in the room. Nothing felt real. He was reading to his father, and that was something he'd never thought he could do.

He stumbled then over the last few words. His tongue became confused, and he rushed to get out the final syllables. Even after he was finished, he stared at the page.

"Splendid," Phillip English said quietly.

"Aye. He's a fine student," Joseph Putnam said.

"What say you to that, Joseph?" Phillip said to Papa.

When Papa didn't say anything, Mr. English quickly turned to the tray of cider mugs and gaily handed one to young

Putnam as he talked, too loudly, Josiah thought. Josiah closed the book and looked down at his boots. It was then that he saw the white linen napkin sticking out of the waist of his britches.

Almost gasping, Josiah looked quickly at Papa. His back was turned as he gazed out the window. With shaking fingers, Josiah tucked the napkin into his britches, just as Papa turned to look at him. He felt his cheeks blazing.

"Twenty-six more villagers were elected to the church at Salem Village this week," Papa said. "I, of course, was not among them."

Josiah's head spun, but he nodded. *What was he talking about?*

"It's all part of a plan, y'see, to get independence from the town for Salem Village. Those of us who don't believe in it are being excluded from God's own church. But it's an independence they're not ready for, because not a one of them can read. Not a one of them even knows what is happening in their own colony." His sandy, brooding eyebrows came together in a frown. "People like the Putnams, except for young Joseph, of course, are afraid of the light of knowledge among their plain citizens. They are afraid of people like you, Josiah."

The room became still, and once again Joseph Hutchinson held out his hand, and once again Josiah went to stand under it as it came softly down on his shoulder. As his father squeezed it tenderly, he looked down at his son, and Josiah saw the pride shining in his eyes.

But Josiah wasn't proud. He wanted to blurt out, *But I'm*

*a thief! I've done wrong and I have to pay to keep it quiet
by being a thief—stealing from Mr. English himself!*

Maybe, he thought for the tiniest second—maybe his father
would understand that he hadn't really thought it was wrong
to go aboard the *Adventure* until Simon told him so. But the
second passed, as it had with Joseph Putnam, as it had even
with God. No one could know.

"Would I could feel so proud of your sister now," Papa said.

Phillip English handed each of them a cup of cider.
"What's this? Young Hope has disappointed you in some way?
I cannot believe it!"

"Aye, well, 'tis a puzzle," Papa said.

Josiah set his mug on the table and waited.

"She was late for her evening work one day. Came runnin'
in all aflush, and the first thing my wife saw was—" he looked
around as if it were painful to say the rest "—was a gold chain
around her neck. Now I know, Phillip, that you do not share
the Puritan thought that bedecking oneself with jewels sepa-
rates a person from God—but it wasn't the wearin' of a bauble
that made me angry. It was the lie she told."

"I cannot believe that beautiful young girl would lie,
Joseph," Phillip said.

Josiah found himself shaking his head, too. Hope may have
done her share of slipping around unnoticed, but when she
had to answer, she was always honest.

"When I asked her where it came from, she looked down
at it as if she'd never seen the thing before. Her face even
went white, and she said she didn't know where it came
from."

"Perhaps that's the truth," Phillip said.

"Ach! It's a chain as big around as an earthworm, and shinin' gold it is. You tell me how such a thing gets 'round your neck and you don't even know it!"

"How does she explain it?"

Papa looked into his mug. "She says she fell asleep in a cabin in the woods, and when she awoke she ran home for fear of trouble for bein' late."

"You can't entirely doubt her story," Phillip said, and added gently, "you know she cannot hear well. Perhaps someone did approach her—"

"Who would do such a thing?"

Josiah riveted his eyes to his cider mug to keep from crying out, *I know! I know!* He knew the gold chain. He'd seen one in Mr. English's shop. And he'd seen one around the neck of Ann Putnam. But should he say anything when he didn't know for sure? When he didn't know what was happening back in the village between Hope and her enemies?

"'Tis still a mystery," Papa said.

"You haven't whipped the girl have you, Joseph?" Phillip English asked.

Papa shook his head. "Nay. I've not whipped my children for some time. I've taken to reading the sermons of Cotton Mather—an old friend of yours," he said to young Putnam. "He says children are sinful by nature, but he opposes punishment by the rod, and I am agreed. And yet—"

He didn't offer to tell what punishment he had given to Hope, and no one asked. Talk turned to other things, and Josiah sighed heavily. If he wasn't lost in the fog before, he surely was now. He knew so many secrets—and he couldn't tell any of them.

＋ ＋ ＋

Chapter Twelve

is father was already off doing business with Phillip English when Josiah arrived in the schoolroom the next morning. Joseph Putnam wasn't there yet, and Josiah slunk miserably into his chair and toyed with an alphabet block.

He hadn't slept well. None of the things that usually put him to sleep seemed to work anymore. If he looked over the memories of the day, his sins haunted him like bad dreams. If he tried to imagine himself as a ship's captain on the high seas, he could only think of how impossible that would be if everyone found out what he was doing. And if he even thought of praying, he could only remember that God must be disappointed in him. Josiah had pushed Him too far away to be able to go to Him now.

"A schilling for your thoughts, Captain," Joseph Putnam said softly. Josiah hadn't heard him come in, and he tried to smile.

"That is not a real smile." Joseph set his pile of books down and sat across from Josiah. His eyes were sad, Josiah thought. "We've become good friends, have we not, Captain?"

"Aye."

"Then I may speak freely?"

Josiah nodded nervously.

"I've noticed from time to time, as we've studied together, that you sometimes seem troubled. You're a bright young man, and I've told myself you can probably solve any problem that comes your way." He leaned forward, and his eyes pulled Josiah's in with a gentle tug. "But last night I saw that you are truly disturbed by something—something you don't want even your father to know."

Josiah could hear the voices crying in his head, *Tell him! He is your friend! Tell him!*

"I cannot think that you would trust me more than your father," Joseph went on. "So I won't ask you to tell me what it is that weighs so heavily on your mind. But I do know you're frightened, and I wonder—" He stopped and studied his hands for a moment, as if the next few words were written there. "I wonder if you remember that story about Jonah I read to you from the Bible some time ago."

"Aye," Josiah said in a voice even he could barely hear.

"You remember that Jonah was afraid of what God wanted him to do, so he ran away. But the farther he tried to run from God, the more trouble he got into."

"He was sw—swallowed by a fish," Josiah mumbled.

Joseph chuckled softly. "Before you are gulped down, Captain, go back to God. He can set you free to do what is right."

Josiah's eyes filled with tears. He wanted to tell him now,

but his throat was too clogged with sobs. Joseph put a hand softly on his arm. "Tell me the bravest thing you ever did."

Josiah swallowed hard and blinked against the tears. "I—I once—I saved my sister's life—"

"And I'm sure to do that you had to take great risks, eh?"

"Aye."

"Why were you able to do that?"

"Because I knew—I knew it was—the right thing."

Joseph nodded slowly. "When it's the right thing, God takes care of you. When you know it isn't—you must go to Him and find out what is."

Josiah looked down at the tabletop, and tears blurred his eyes again. Suddenly, he felt warm fingers under his chin. Joseph tilted Josiah's head up with the only rough gesture Josiah had ever seen him make.

"Nothing gets done that way, Captain," he said, almost sternly. "Hangin' your head is what brings you trouble to begin with."

Josiah stared at him. He wasn't surprised to hear that. He'd heard it before—from Hope.

Hope. She was at home with trouble of her own—trouble he could help her out of, if he were only brave enough.

But there were other things to do first. He wasn't sure how he was going to do them yet—or if he could do them—but he knew now that at least he would try.

Joseph Putnam discovered some "unexpected business" he had to take care of, and with a wink he told Josiah that the afternoon's class was canceled. His father left after dinner

with a pat on the shoulder and a proud smile that made
Josiah shrink again with shame. *But you won't be disap-
pointed in me, Papa,* Josiah thought as he watched him go.
At least—I hope you won't.

While Mrs. English and the babies slept, Josiah went to his
room and knelt before the window. A moist, delicious breeze
was blowing off the harbor, and Josiah tried to imagine that
God Himself rode it into his room. He was close now, and
Josiah began to pray. It had been a long time. There was
much catching up to do.

At supper, Josiah nibbled on a piece of bread and waited
for the sun to begin to set.

"Your mother will believe I never fed you these six weeks," Mary
English said to him. "Hannah and Judith eat more than you do!"

"I'm not hungered now," he said, "but I would like to take
a macaroon for later, if you please."

"Why, of course! Would you like a package prepared for
your evening walk perhaps?"

Josiah's eyes widened, and he didn't trust himself to speak.
He nodded politely.

"Very well, then. I shall speak to Cook."

His eyes met Joseph Putnam's across the table. He didn't
know everything, Josiah thought, but he understood.

"Now if we are finished talking about the boy's appetite,"
Phillip English said good-naturedly, "I would like to announce
that I have found a new captain for the *Adventure*. He was
unhappy working for Captain Hollingsworth and has agreed
to come aboard with us. She's to set sail next week."

Everyone cheered, Josiah loudest of all. That meant Simon would be out to sea, where he would get his food from another cook. Perhaps he didn't have to do this tonight, after all. But he pushed that thought away. He had already promised God.

When supper was over, Josiah went to the study and tapped lightly on the door.

"Mr. English," he said from the doorway, "I'm off for a walk."

Mr. English got up and parted the curtain to look out. "There's a storm brewing, Josiah. The barometer is dropping, and those high clouds are closing in. We've been preparing for it all afternoon. We even had to raise the Blue Peter and put the—" His voice faded, and then his eyes came back to Josiah. "Well, you want to be off, don't you, lad? You'd best take a jacket. There's one of mine on a peg in the back hallway, eh? Use that. And see you return before it begins to blow, eh?"

"Aye."

He ran to the back hall and found a jacket with pouches inside. The sleeves hung below his hands, but the jacket would protect him from the wind. Then he stopped by the kitchen, where Cook had two bundles of macaroons large enough to feed the whole *Adventure* crew ready for him.

"These are not all for me," Josiah told her.

"It matters not to me who eats them," Cook said. And she went back to sanding the trenchers.

Josiah was stunned for a minute. Might it be that they never would have cared at all that he—

But he shook his head and hurried out. If he were to beat the storm, he would have to be quick about it.

Once out of sight of the English house, Josiah broke into a run, whipping past the houses and the shops on English's Lane. By the time he reached the warehouse, the shelf of high clouds that Mr. English had talked about had closed in on the harbor completely, and they were blacker than the night that was soon to follow. After all of his trips to the wharf in the evenings, Josiah could tell that the wind was blowing from a different direction than usual. It whipped into the east, and Josiah clutched the big jacket around him to keep the macaroons from blowing off with it. It even started to rain as he headed toward the wharf, an angrier rain than what fell in the afternoons every few days. But, in the midst of this wind-driven nastiness, Josiah stopped short.

The galleon was gone!

Josiah wiped the water from his eyebrows and looked again. The braces that had held her on the wharf as Juan and the other shipbuilders had hammered and sawed and planed and painted were still there, but the stately ship had disappeared.

But there was no time to wonder about it. The storm Phillip English had warned of was here. Even as he ran through the driving bullets of rain toward the *Adventure*'s dock, he saw the choppy waters biting at the pilings. Then, just as he reached the dock, two things crashed on him at once.

The *Adventure* wasn't there.

And a noise like the roar of a woods full of bears was rolling in from the open ocean.

Josiah ran to the end of the dock, but the ship was truly gone—disappeared just like the galleon. As the roar grew louder, Josiah looked up, and a scream caught in his throat.

The sea seemed to have gathered itself up in one raging gray wave, and it was barreling toward him at the back of the wind.

Spinning on his heel and slipping on the wet planks, Josiah tore up the dock and across the wharf. The rain poured down in torrents now, and the wind seemed ready to swallow him up in its fierce jaws. The noise was deafening as the wave crashed over the dock behind him. It was a wonder he heard the voice when it called out.

"Here, farm boy! Over here!"

Simon was tearing toward him in the rain, his soaked coat flying behind him. Without explanation, he grabbed Josiah in the usual grip and dragged him toward the water.

"No!" Josiah screamed. "I've brought it! I've brought it!"

It occurred to him even then that to drown him for food seemed like a drastic move, but when Simon yanked him down one of the docks, Josiah saw where they were headed. He felt everything inside him stop.

They were about to board the galleon.

She was moored on a dock directly across from where she'd been built, and the rain and the wind formed a stormy curtain around her that kept Josiah from seeing her before. She looked smaller and more fragile now as she tossed helplessly on the black, furious waves. Josiah was sure she would be dashed against the rocks and destroyed before she ever got out to sea.

The gangplank rocked crazily as they crossed it, and Josiah found himself clinging to Simon. Once aboard, Simon shook him off and held him at arm's length. All around them sailors dashed madly about, and no one seemed to notice or care that Josiah was there.

"Go below—to the cargo hold—and wait for me there," Simon shouted. "Go aft until you—"

"I know!" Josiah shouted back. He had studied a diagram of a Spanish galleon in Sir Henry's book a hundred times. He knew how to get to the cargo hold.

Once there, though, he wished he'd never found it. The storm seemed to pick up the galleon and hurl her from one wave to another in big angry passes that shook her framework and threw Josiah all over the hold. Within minutes, his head throbbed from being banged around, and his stomach was upside down. The place to be in a storm was on the decks, Sir Henry had said. There you could roll with the pitching and tossing and not get seasick.

Josiah hung onto whatever he could find until he got to the hatch. Climbing the two sets of ladders that led topside was like trying to ride an unbroken horse, and Josiah was on his hands and knees when he reached the forecastle deck. He crawled to the side and looked around for a place to hide.

"Anchors aweigh!" he heard someone cry.

The order was repeated down the deck until two sailors within steps of Josiah began to turn the capstan, and the thick rope began to move.

Anchors aweigh! Josiah screamed silently. *No!*

But as he watched in horror, the noble galleon was put out to sea for the first time.

✠ ⚜ ✠

Chapter Thirteen

Josiah plastered himself against the bulkhead. Men rushed around him, their clothes drenched and clinging to their skins. Shouts shot back and forth.

"The forecastle's awash! Start bailin' her out!"

"We must needs sail ahull—the wind'll rip her sheets!"

"Lash the helm alee!"

Before his eyes, sailors hauled huge lines to and from the 12 standing structures on the deck that housed the sheaves for pulling the lines in and out. Josiah had read once that the sailors called them Apostles because there were 12 of them, but he thought little about that now. His thoughts were as confused as the shouts that caught in the wind and were carried away.

The galleon's going to sea! Is she ready? Will she wreck? Will she sink? Who is her captain?

One huge blast of wind and wave pulled the galleon

straight up on end, and Josiah slid in several inches of racing water up against one of the Apostles. The ship had no sooner righted itself when a shout went up from the crew. Josiah caught only the word "breach" before a wave as high as his house broke over the deck, and Josiah came up sputtering and choking. There was no time to think about the trouble he would be in *now*—if he ever returned to land.

"Out of the way, boy!" someone shouted.

Josiah looked down to find that both of his arms were wrapped around one of the Apostles. He pulled them off and hid behind the sheave.

From above, someone shouted something in urgent Spanish.

Josiah's head jerked upward. High above him, swaying from the mizzenmast, was Juan. His black hair hung in dripping strings around his face, a face that was pinched with danger.

The sailor beside Josiah shook his head in confusion. Juan made a frantic motion with his arms, but the sailor only looked back, bewildered.

"He's telling you to lock the sheave on that line or the line will pull free and those sails will fly out and rip apart!"

Josiah's heart stopped. The person shouting the message and striding toward them on the slippery deck was Phillip English.

Josiah crouched hard behind the Apostle. He'd planned to tell Mr. English the whole truth tomorrow—but not now. He *mustn't* find him now.

Above his head, the sailor rocked back the sheave and then

took off aft where someone else was shouting. Josiah peeked over the top. Phillip English held onto the bulkhead and watched Juan while his hand shielded his eyes from the rain that hammered his face. Josiah ducked again and squeezed his eyes shut. *God—please—I'm trying—please don't let him find me here—please let the ship be safe—please—*

Before he could even say "Amen," another angry swell swept over the deck and Josiah tumbled in its roll. Then, as quickly as it was pushed over him, the water was sucked away. Josiah lay on the deck like a flounder. Above him, Juan hurled a stream of frenzied Spanish words and jabbed the air with his finger.

Josiah's head jerked to where he pointed. The sheave was beginning to move, and with it, the line that held the sail safely in place. If it rolled much more, the line would come loose, and with it the sail. "That sail will fly out and rip apart!" Phillip English cried.

Josiah looked up once more at Juan. His face was purple with shouting. He looked down at the sheave. It was slipping fast.

Josiah grabbed the Apostle's post and hauled himself upward. He took hold of the handle that operated the sheave and held on.

It stopped turning, but Josiah's hands were slippery and his muscles burned. He couldn't hold it for long, and he wasn't strong enough to yank it back and lock it into place. Helplessly he searched for Juan's face.

"I can't!" Josiah screamed. "I can't hold it!"

And then a pair of firm, gloved hands covered his. "Pull

with me!" Phillip English cried.

Together, hands clenched and faces twisted, Josiah and Mr. English pulled—until the sheave was locked in place, and with it, the sail.

Almost as suddenly as it had whipped up its strength, the storm began to weaken, or so it seemed to Josiah. After Phillip English rushed away from him and toward the quarter-deck, Josiah held on tightly to the handle and to his own footing. Almost at that instant, the galleon began to scud over the water and career out to sea. They sailed ahull—without sails—for what seemed like a day. Then Josiah watched two sailors let down the anchor and they moored far out of the harbor, rocking and pitching, but safe.

As Josiah looked toward land, he saw the storm still raging in the harbor. Out here the rain poured and the wind blew, but the sea was not as angry in these deeper waters. Josiah remembered Sir Henry, writing of taking moored ships out to sea a ways in a storm and anchoring them there, lest they be dashed against the rocks and destroyed. That, he realized, was why the *Adventure* was gone, too, and her new captain was there to save her. Phillip English had even told him they'd raised the Blue Peter, to call the crew back to the ship.

He didn't dare move from his spot, even after the rain gave way to a miserable mist and the wind died down to a few exhausted puffs. It was there that Phillip English found him.

"Come along, son," was all he said.

Josiah's heart had stopped thrashing around in his chest and the fear no longer raced through his veins, but a sickening uneasiness settled in his stomach as he followed Mr. English below. They wove through several passageways until Phillip opened a hatch and nodded for Josiah to enter.

They went into a shiny, tidy cabin with a brass porthole and a box-hammock hanging from the overhead. Josiah knew it must be the captain's cabin, but he was too miserable to be excited. He stood in one corner and hung his head—but then he brought his chin up. *Hangin' your head is what brings you trouble to begin with,* a voice seemed to whisper.

He peered through his dripping curls at Phillip English and waited.

"You must get out of those wet clothes," Mr. English said. "You'll be sick abed and your papa will have my hide, eh?"

Josiah stared.

"Come on, then. Off with them. Wrap yourself in this."

Mr. English reached up to the hammock and pulled down a woolen blanket. Then he pulled off his own wet clothes and wrapped himself in a large cloak. Josiah still stood frozen for a minute and then began to peel away the jacket. One sleeve stuck stubbornly to his arm. When he tugged at it, a wet linen napkin plopped to the deck and splatted its soggy contents across the cabin. Phillip English eyed it sharply and looked up at Josiah.

There is no choice now, Josiah told himself. *It is time for the truth.*

Slowly, Josiah pulled out the other ruined packet of maca-roons and held it out to Mr. English. To his surprise, the man laughed.

"No, thank you, Josiah!" he said. "That ride gave my stomach a bit of a tumble. I'm surely not hungered—"

"No—sir!" Josiah blurted out. "I—I came to the wharf tonight—to give these to—to someone—as my last payment."

Phillip English tilted his head, elegant even when it was dripping wet. "Payment?"

"Aye. And then I was going to come home and—and—tell you the truth—no matter what you decided to do—because—because to lie—to lie and cover it up is worse than—than the mistake I made in the first place."

Phillip English reached out and put his hand on Josiah's shoulder. "Perhaps you should start from the beginning, eh?" he said quietly.

So Josiah did. He told him everything—about sneaking aboard the *Adventure* and getting his foot caught in the sheave. About the rat and Simon and the threat of being exposed. He even described himself stealing food from Mr. English's table and coming to the wharf every night to make his payments.

Josiah was shaking when he was finished, but more with relief than fear. For through it all, Phillip English had listened quietly and nodded his head, and his eyes were full of understanding, not anger. He didn't want to think of what his father's face would look like when he was told, so he didn't. He just thought of how light he now felt, with this burden lifted from his shoulders.

"Josiah," Phillip English said, "I knew all along that you were taking walks to the wharf every night."

"Aye. I saw that when my—when my father came and you said—"

"And was I angry with you?"

"No," Josiah said meekly.

"Nor was I angry with you for going aboard the *Adventure*, that day or any other."

Josiah felt his mouth dropping open.

Mr. English nodded. "Your father told Juan to watch out for you when you came, and he did. Every time he saw you on the wharf, he told me, so I would know you were safe."

"But—but Juan does not—he doesn't speak English!"

"No," said Mr. English, smiling, "but he understands it. And I speak Spanish."

That explained so many things, and Josiah's head spun with all of them. But Phillip English went on.

"You see, lad, you were welcome to explore any of the ships, anything in the warehouse, anytime you wanted to. That is why your father sent you here—so that even at your tender age you could begin to know about choices besides farming. He knows the society we live in is changing, and he is doing everything he can to prepare you for that." He sighed. "It is sad, but even my little girls will have to grow up faster than I would wish, simply because there are surprising changes coming, and you must all be ready for them."

Tears threatened to climb into Josiah's eyes. "Why—why didn't someone tell me that it was all right to—for me—"

"Because, my boy," Phillip English said kindly, "you never asked."

As Josiah tried to take that in, Phillip scooped up the messy macaroons from the cabin deck and smiled. "Now then, there is business to attend to. Suppose you get out of those clothes once and for all and get yourself wrapped in that blanket. And wait you here—I shall return."

Josiah's now half-dry clothes were so stuck to his skin, stripping them off was like removing husks from a cob of corn. Finally, he had them all in a pile and was pulling the blanket around him when the hatch opened. He yanked the blanket closer around him—for Phillip English pushed Simon into the cabin.

The tall young seaman's hair stuck out from his head like red thorns, and his clothes were twisted and glued to his skinny frame. He looked comical, but anger glittered in his eyes.

"I believe you have something to say to Mr. Hutchinson," Phillip English said.

Simon nodded sulkily, his eyes still gleaming at Josiah.

"Good, then," said Mr. English. "Let you say it. I shall return in a few moments' time to settle my own business with you."

And to Josiah's horror, he turned and left, closing the hatch behind him.

For the shortest of seconds, Josiah's heart started to pound, and that old sick feeling of dread began to make its way up to his throat.

But then Simon made a mistake. He threw back his red head, and he laughed.

All fear shivered out of Josiah at that moment, and in its place came anger—anger bigger than anything that could flash from Simon's eyes.

"I find—I see nothing funny," Josiah said.

"Well, I surely do, farm boy! You run and whine to the great Mr. English about how I trapped you into stealing for me—and then he leaves *you* to face me—all alone." Simon let out another laugh that sounded like the cackle of one of the Hutchinson hens.

But the boy Simon had trapped in the hold of the *Adventure* was a somewhat different boy from the one he faced here now. Josiah squared his shoulders—and remembered to tilt his chin up.

"I came here tonight to tell you that the—the mac-mac-macaroons I brought were my good—good-bye gift. I wasn't going to bring you—any—any more treats because it didn't matter anymore—I was going to tell—tell—Mr. English and everyone what happened—myself."

Simon snorted. "You're a liar. You got caught aboard this ship because I dragged you on, and you had no choice but to tell."

Josiah shrugged, surprising even himself. "Think—think as you will—but I know what—what I've said is—is the truth."

Simon studied Josiah's eyes for a moment. It was probably the first time he'd ever really looked into them. Usually they were riveted to his boots whenever Simon was around. Finally, he scowled.

"Doesn't matter. I'd had my fill of sweets anyway—and I'll be off to sea on the *Adventure* next week, now they've found a captain."

"You think Mr. English—Mr. English will still let you go?"

Simon sneered. "And why shouldn't he? This was a—what do they always call it—a boyish prank. I'll be whipped or something and then—off I go—"

"Not when he—when he knows—you—you have his—boatswain's pipe."

Simon's face drained. He didn't even open his mouth to

protest, because as his eyes met Josiah's the truth clinked like the set of a sheave. It was only a guess—that the gold, bejeweled boatswain's pipe was in the bulging pouch, *his* pouch. But now Josiah knew he was right.

Simon quickly gathered his shoulders up. "And who, may I ask, is going to tell him?"

Josiah smiled innocently. "Oh—you are!"

Simon's shocked expression melted to laughter, and he gasped as he grabbed his sides. "I am!" he said, snorting and snuffling. "In some moment of madness, perhaps—"

"No." Josiah put his hand up. "I can tell—I can tell you how it's—it's done. First you go to God—He'll tell you what—what was right all along—because—because you'll stop feeling—feeling afraid, and you'll get—you—you'll be peaceful. Then you go to Mr. English—and—and the words will—will just come because—y'see—you don't have trouble—trouble talking like—like I do."

Instead of answering, Simon took several steps toward Josiah. His eyes narrowed as he came closer. "And how, *Reverend* Farm Boy Hutchinson, will you know if I've told him?"

"Tomorrow," Josiah said, "tomorrow—I shall ask him."

With a jerk of his arm, Simon slashed Josiah across the face. Before it even began to sting, he grabbed the younger boy by the arm and shoved him against the cabin wall.

It wasn't the almost-playful grab Simon usually used to push Josiah around. It was a hard grip, a painful one. One he'd felt before—

"You intend to ask him, eh?" Simon growled through his teeth. "Eh?"

"Yes!" Josiah said. Spittle drops hissed out with the *S* and landed on Simon's cheek. With all his might, Josiah threw back his head and spit again into Simon's eyes, a mouthful this time.

Simon screwed his eyes shut, and his hold loosened. Josiah wrenched himself free and dove for the hatch.

"Come here, you stupid—! I'll whip the devil out of you!"

Josiah hit the deck on his belly with Simon on top of him, his arms around Josiah's throat. Josiah gasped and jabbed his elbow upward—into Simon's ribs. As he flinched, Josiah rolled as hard as he could. Like two snarling bear cubs they rolled together, first to one side of the cabin and then to the other. The blanket flew off and Josiah was left in his drawers, but he didn't stop. He grabbed and punched and bit with a fury that felt nothing but its own hot anger. And as he clawed and scratched, a memory popped crazily into his head. A memory of two bodies rolling beside a wagon. A memory of cries and curses and a final moan of pain.

As if he were part of that memory, Josiah brought his knee up and shoved it, as hard as he could, into Simon's stomach. Simon gasped and flopped onto his back. Josiah scrambled to his knees and backed away, but his kneecap came down on something hard.

Beside him lay a chunky gold ring with an S raised on its shiny surface.

"What are you about here?" cried a voice from the hatch.

Phillip English stormed into the cabin with Juan behind him. Josiah got to his feet, still breathing hard. When he looked down, the ring was gone.

"Are you mad, boy?" Phillip shouted at Simon. Simon had by now stood up, and Josiah saw his pouch swinging, as usual, from Simon's waist.

"You should be ashamed, throwin' yourself on a boy half your size," Phillip English said.

"He—!"

"He what?" Phillip said.

Simon clamped his jaws firmly and stared at the deck.

"As I thought," Phillip said. "Juan, get him out of my sight, please."

Juan took Simon by the arm and gave him a push toward the hatch. Simon looked back only once, his colorless eyes in resentful slits, slicing through Josiah.

Phillip English shook his head and ran a hand through his hair. "What possesses a boy to behave like that? It must be the devil himself."

"Is—is Simon really an orphan?" Josiah asked.

Phillip looked at him quickly. "Aye."

Josiah didn't say anything else. He put his hand to his cheek and drew it back smeared with blood. Once he thought he'd seen Simon almost friendly, chomping on tarts and watching the fog and having someone to talk to. But he was wrong. There was probably not a friendly bone in Simon's body. It was good, then, that he was out of his life forever. Or so he hoped.

✢ ◦✢◦ ✢

Chapter Fourteen

The next few weeks flew by and with them the last of summer. Josiah kept his routine—school all day with Joseph Putnam, supper with the English family, the wharf and the ships in the evenings. On Sundays his father came to Salem Town for Meeting, but Hope and his mother stayed behind in the village. He knew it had something to do with the trouble Hope was in, but he didn't ask.

There were a few differences now. In the afternoons, instead of Joseph reading to him from the Bible, he now read to Joseph. It was hard at first. "They spoke—they spoke so strangely back then!" Josiah would wail. But when Joseph found the stories for him, Josiah was drawn in and the words came more easily.

"Have you taken note of something?" Joseph said one afternoon when he'd finished reading.

"What?"

"What doesn't happen when you read aloud that happens when you speak your own words?"

Josiah considered that for a minute, and then he felt his face light up. "I don't—stutter."

"Ah," Joseph Putnam said, smiling. "Then we know it can be done, eh?"

The other difference in Josiah's routine was that now after supper when he flew out of the English house, down English's Lane, and out onto the Point of Rocks, he didn't have to look behind him, afraid someone would see him and demand to know what he was about there.

He remembered his wish to make friends with Shipwright Juan, and now he always stopped to talk to him and deliver a macaroon or a sliver of pie carefully wrapped in a napkin. With his few remaining teeth, Juan chewed and smiled and bobbed his head. The galleon was finished now, and he had only to do the finishing touches. Josiah watched Juan one evening, just as the sun was setting over the calm harbor. As Josiah sprawled on his belly on the dock, Juan painted the name on the galleon's hull. Slowly, carefully, the letters came into view.

H-U-T-C-H-I-N-S-O-N.

When the last stroke was done, Juan smiled at Josiah. Josiah smiled back. In so many ways, she *was* his ship.

Another evening, not long after the storm, Josiah saw that the *Adventure* was gone again, and he knew this time she was far out to sea, carrying her precious treasures to the West Indies. With a sigh of relief, he thought of Simon.

Josiah knew little of what had happened to Simon after

that night. He saw Mr. English with his boatswain's pipe the next day, and he heard Phillip tell his wife he had found it in the warehouse building—someone had slid it under the door to his office. Josiah was disappointed that Simon hadn't done the right thing and confessed, but he wasn't surprised. Perhaps Simon had indeed gotten off with a whipping for what he had done to Josiah and was on his way to the Caribbean even now.

But as Josiah wandered down the wharf toward the *Adventure*'s empty dock, he saw a tall, thin silhouette against the sunset. Even the spikes of the figure's hair were outlined in black, and Josiah knew it was Simon.

He sat on a rock beside the dock, legs crossed in front of him, staring out to sea. Josiah knew he'd wanted so much to go on the next voyage. He also knew Simon wanted to be a sailor even more than he did. Simon had nothing else—no scarf other than the fog, no real friends other than the boys he bullied during Meeting, no father to go to even when he was wrong and confused.

For a moment Josiah wanted to go sit next to him. He even took a few steps forward. After all, he had no reason to be frightened of him now.

Or did he? Josiah rubbed his bruised arm. He remembered the gold ring that had bounced across the deck of the captain's cabin that night—and then disappeared. He remembered all the things Simon had stolen—the food, the boatswain's pipe—and what else?

Slowly, Josiah backed up and crept quietly away. Someone could probably help Simon. But it couldn't be him.

The air was more crisp in the mornings now, and the evenings chillier and windier. One day Joseph Putnam cleared his throat and said, "Captain, our time together here in Salem Town is drawing to a close."

Josiah felt his heart sink.

"I'm somewhat saddened by it, too," he said. "You are by far the best student I have ever had."

Josiah grinned. "I am the *only* student you have ever had!"

Joseph's eyes twinkled. "Aye—I can never fool you, Captain. But—" He stopped and wiggled his eyebrows. "You may not be the last. In fact, you may be my student again."

Josiah's eyes widened.

"Aye. You see, the time for my wedding is fast approaching."

Joseph stopped. Josiah hadn't meant to show the cloud that had passed over his thoughts just then, but Joseph always watched him so closely.

"What is it, Captain?" he said.

"I—it's not my business, of course—"

"Of course—"

"But—don't marry Constance Porter! It's a trap!"

Joseph bit his lip, but his eyes were dancing. Josiah knew he wanted to laugh.

"It isn't a joke!" Josiah cried. "It's—they want—it's all the money, and the plan to take over—"

Joseph put his hand on Josiah's shoulder. "I am marrying Constance because I love her. I want to build a life with her. Young as she is, I know she'll make a good wife." He leaned back in his chair and studied his hands for a moment. "There are some will look at the match we've made and shake their heads and say, 'Ah, they've married for money.' Or, 'They've married as part of some devious plot!'" Joseph threw his handsome oak-colored head back and laughed brightly. "I let them say as they will, Captain. Only I know what I do, eh?"

Josiah nodded, and inside a tiny pinched part began to let loose. He should have known all along that Joseph Putnam would only do what was right and never let other people make his decisions for him. He had taught Josiah himself that.

"But that is not my point," Joseph went on. "When Constance and I are married, I plan to make my way in Salem Village. I will have land there, after all, and there's a good deal to be done there, including the schooling of a village full of unruly young boys. Will you help me get them into shape, Captain?"

A smile sprang up on Josiah's face. "Aye!"

"Then we'd best both be getting back to Salem Village soon, eh?"

Josiah nodded, and suddenly a torrent of confusing feelings began to tumble inside him. There was so much here he would be sad to leave. But Salem Village was his home, and he missed her trees and farms and smells—and even William and Ezekiel. And, of course, Mama and Papa—

Josiah struggled with that one. To his knowledge nothing was said to his father about the mistakes he'd made here. Phillip English was forgiving. Joseph Putnam had understood. But would his father? Were they keeping it from him for fear of what he might do?

And then there was Hope. Thoughts of the gold chain haunted even his dreams. He wanted to help her, but he didn't know how. So he'd seen a gold chain around Ann Putnam's neck. It would be his word against hers. And he'd seen one like it in Phillip English's shop. What did that prove? It was all so jumbled in his mind—as it always seemed to be. Only now, he knew, he could go to God with anything.

"Now, then, before we leave here, is there anything you would like to learn before those other wretched boys join us, eh?" Joseph asked.

Josiah shook his head sadly and looked around the schoolroom. He'd spent many happy hours here, struggling and breaking through and then sailing ahead. When he had first walked in here, words on a page were like Spanish to him. Now he could return home and read the Bible to his father.

Suddenly, though, Josiah had an idea. "There is one thing I want to know before I go."

When he told Joseph Putnam what it was, his teacher nodded and smiled. "That's a fine idea, Captain."

Two days later, Josiah found himself putting his things into his bundle in his room. He and Joseph would leave right after dinner for Salem Village. As he folded his clothes and tucked them inside the cloth bag, he felt something in the bottom. Slowly, he pulled out a blue woolen scarf.

He didn't remember bringing it. Why in the world would he need such a thing in the middle of a Massachusetts summer? Perhaps his mother had put it in—

But it didn't matter. Josiah rolled it up and put it aside.

"Josiah," someone said behind him.

"Aye?"

Phillip English strolled into the room, and behind him Mary and the two babies. Hannah was curled up in her mother's arms, sucking her finger, and Judith hung about her skirts.

"Goo' day!" Judith piped up.

It was the only thing Josiah had ever heard her say. He smiled at her, and as he did, she held out a chubby fist and uncurled her fingers. Josiah stared.

"She has—she has your boatswain's whistle!" he said to Mr. English.

"Aye, but not for long," Phillip said. "Go on, Judith."

The little girl toddled forward and held the golden whistle up to Josiah. Its jewels gleamed in the sun that streamed, as always, into Josiah's room.

Josiah looked blankly at Mr. English.

"It's for you," Phillip said. "My gift for helping to save the *Hutchinson*. You show signs of becoming a fine seaman."

Josiah took the pipe and its chain from Judith and cradled them in his hand. But he looked up at Mr. English and shook his head. "My father will never allow me to wear this. 'Tis against our beliefs."

"Then do as you like with it," he said. "Perhaps you'll keep it until you have your own ship, eh? Or carry it in that pouch I've seen you with. Where is that?"

He glanced at Josiah's waist, and Josiah felt his cheeks redden.

"I—I gave it to Simon, sir," he said.

"Simon!"

"Well—he has—he has nothing—I think—I think that's why he—does the things he does—"

"You're a generous boy," Mary English said. "You deserve a fine gift. Go on, then. Take it."

"Our abundance comes from God," Phillip said quietly. "We have naught to do but share it with others."

When they left the room, Josiah sat on the edge of the bed and stared for a while at the pipe that by some miracle had replaced his stolen wooden whistle. The thoughts raced around in his head, but they weren't jumbled this time. He ran to the window and looked up at the sun. He still had some time before dinner, and there were two things he needed to do.

With a mysterious bundle tucked under his shirt, Josiah left the house and ran down to the wharf. Sailors scurried back and forth as always, but Josiah couldn't find the person he was looking for. He hurried to the shipyard, where Juan had already started on a new vessel for Mr. English.

"I've come to say good-bye," Josiah said.

Juan's black eyes drooped, and he nodded sadly.

"I shall be back though! I—I intend to become a sailor myself!"

Juan nodded happily then and Josiah nodded, too. He reached inside his shirt and brought out the woolen scarf. "Juan, if you—if it so happens—should you see Simon about—would you give him this, please?"

Juan cocked his head and frowned, but Josiah pushed the scarf into his hands. "He's a scoundrel—I know. But even scoundrels—even they—they must stay warm, eh?" Josiah grinned, and he formed his next words carefully. "Juan— adíos, mi amigo."

Juan's dried-berry teeth came into view and he bobbed his head. "Good-bye, my friend."

The sun was getting higher in the sky now, and Josiah ran hard to reach English's Lane for his last stop. He stopped to catch his breath on the step of the shop. If he were to help Hope when he got home, he had to check something one more time.

As he straightened to go in, the shop door flew open and a tall figure jumped straight from the doorway into the lane, skipping the steps entirely. His long legs carried him easily and quickly down the lane and toward the wharf. Josiah couldn't see his face, but he did see his red hair sticking up in spikes from his head.

Josiah sprang into the shop. The old shopkeeper was panting angrily and mumbling to himself as he poked around at the shelf where Josiah had seen the gold chain. He looked up with fire in his faded eyes, but when he saw Josiah he turned back to his work.

"It's you, then—well, come in," he said. "But I'll not let that scoundrel in this shop again! I'll tell Mr. English—I refuse to work here if I must have the likes of him!"

"What happened?"

The old man eyed the shelf one more time and shook his head. "Nothing—not this time. I ran him off afore he had a chance to steal me blind again, I did."

Josiah stared. "Has he—did he steal from you before?"

"I've no proof, and that's the truth of it—but I know—" He tapped his wrinkled forehead with his finger. "I know, d'y'see?"

Josiah nodded. He did see.

The old man turned away, still grumbling, and Josiah stepped close to the shelf. The gold chain was still there, and Josiah stared at it long and hard. When he was sure the memory of it was engraved in his brain, he left the shop.

✢ ✦ ✢

Chapter Fifteen

osiah, you've naught to inhale it. There's plenty more
when you've done with that plateful."

Josiah looked up sheepishly from his trencher and felt
droplets of stew running down his chin. His mother smiled
at him, and he grinned back. As delicious as the food was at
the English house, it was good to be back at his own table,
eating Mama's cooking.

It was quiet at the table, but it was a comfortable quiet.
Everyone looked at him as if they'd forgotten what he looked
like while he was away. Twice he caught Hope cocking her
head at him curiously and observing him out of the corner of
her eye. But when he looked back, her eyes darted away.

There was something different about Hope. She seemed
pulled inside herself, Josiah decided, as if talking happily and
watching everything with bright alert eyes the way she usually
did would bring her out into the open where people could

point their fingers at her. When Josiah did see a gleam in her eyes, it looked like anger.

When supper was over, Mama and Hope cleared away the trenchers and mugs, and Papa went to his chair where he sat with his head back and his eyes closed. The windows were open to let in the evening breeze, and from outside Josiah heard the sounds of the farm—the leaves brushing together, the cows mooing softly in the pasture, the chickens cackling lazily after each other. As he turned the table for Mama, he looked about the room. His bedchamber and his schoolroom at the English house were elegant and private. He'd learned a lot there. But this—this was home. Here he knew every crack and knothole, every fly and candlewick. Here, in this place, he had to live all those things he'd learned.

Without a word, he went into the best room and picked up the Bible box. The family Bible was heavy inside as Josiah carried it back to the kitchen. His father looked up with a start.

"That book is not to be touched until it can be read by the one who touches it," his father reminded him.

"Aye." Josiah took the book from its box and cradled it in his lap. Some day he would just hold it and memorize how it felt and smelled when he thumbed through the pages. But now, his fingers moved quickly as he found his place. When he looked up, Papa, Mama, and Hope were all staring at him.

"I will read from second Kings tonight," he said. "Chapter 20 and two."

Mama and Hope still stared, but Papa nodded.

Then, in a clear voice, Josiah began to read to his family. "Josiah was eight years old when he began to reign, and he did that which was right in the sight of the LORD—"

Josiah went on to read how King Josiah's servants found the Book of the Law, and how King Josiah discovered that his people were not following the laws. The king knew God was angry with them, but he asked God's forgiveness and the Lord gave him and his people another chance.

"And the king went up into the house of the LORD," Josiah read, "and all the people, both small and great; and he read in their ears all the words of the book—and the king stood by a pillar, and made a covenant before the LORD, to walk after the LORD, and to keep his commandments—with all his heart—and with all his soul."

When Josiah finished reading he put the Bible back into its box and closed the lid. It was silent in the room, and for a minute Josiah was afraid to look up. Perhaps this idea that Joseph Putnam helped him to prepare for wasn't such a good one, after all. Maybe his father thought he was trying to show off, reading about his namesake—

"Would you be king, Josiah?" his father asked.

"Oh—no sir!" Josiah cried.

But to his surprise, his father nodded and smiled. "Aye, you shall be. Because to be a king, a man must only have wisdom and strength and courage and a love for God. It would appear that you are beginning to find all of those."

The earth must have stopped for a moment—he could see and feel nothing save the pride that shimmered across his father's face.

Hope noticed it, too. Later, when they were in their beds on the second floor, she rolled over and pulled back her curtain to look down into his cot.

"You've made Papa very proud," she said.

"Aye."

"That's good, because he isn't proud of me. I don't think he ever will be again."

Josiah propped himself up on one elbow. "Because of the—gold chain?"

"He's told you, then?"

"Aye. In Salem Town one Sunday. How *did* you get it?"

Hope threw the curtains aside and stood up angrily, towering over him with flashing eyes. "So you don't believe me either, eh? Why can no one trust that what I say is the truth? I went up to the Widow Hooker's cabin—with all the work here, I had so few chances to go there, and when I did I discovered that someone else is now living there."

"Who?"

"I didn't know, but I thought it might be that beggar woman who discovered us there that day, remember? I settled down to wait, so that when she came back I could inform her that that is *our* place." Hope began to pace soundlessly in her bare feet. "But it got late and I fell asleep. When I woke up, it was nearly dark, and I knew I would be in trouble, so I just ran all the way back here." Her face darkened as she passed the window. "If that was my only trouble I would be a happy girl today. I wasn't in this house one minute before Mama discovered that I was wearing a gold chain 'round my neck." Slowly, Hope sank onto the edge of Josiah's cot. "I tell you,

Josiah, I do not know how it got there. I can only guess that it was placed on me while I slept, but no one will believe me. They all want to think that I—I—took it from someplace. Why would I do that and then come prancing home with it swinging from my collar where everyone could see it?"

Josiah nodded. "What did Papa do to you?"

"Nothing. He said he wanted to believe me, my having been raised in a Christian home and all. But until some proof could be found, he didn't know what to do. So I'm a prisoner right here at home. I've gone nowhere since it happened."

"Where is the gold chain now?"

Hope's eyes filled with tears. "Papa keeps it in his pouch 'round his waist—I suppose so he will have it with him if he should find some proof, some explanation—"

"I know where it came from," Josiah said.

Hope's hand froze where she held it, ready to wipe away a tear. "How could you know?"

"The day—the first day I met Joseph Putnam—and—and brought him here, we met—Thomas—Thomas Putnam and Ann on the road on their—on their horses. She leaned over to glare—to glare at me—" Josiah paused to demonstrate, "—and I saw it, spillin'—right out of her collar where she was hidin' it."

Hope searched his face, trying to follow his lips in the darkness. "Did she know you saw it?"

"Nay. When I looked back at her, she had hidden it away again. She didn't want her—her—Thomas Putnam to know—she—she had it."

"Of course not!" Hope's face grew strained. "But, Josiah, where would she get such a thing?"

That was the part Josiah hadn't put together yet. He needed a little more time to figure it out.

When Hope was back in bed and asleep, Josiah tossed on his sheets for a long time. The story was beginning to lose its fuzzy edges in his mind, but some more searching was definitely called for. Knowing what he would do the next day, he fell asleep.

The next day, Giles Porter went back to work for his grandfather, and Josiah was back at his chores again. It had been a long time since he had milked a cow or fed the chickens or pulled the weeds. School, he decided, was much easier than any of this. How had he ever thought otherwise?

By the middle of the afternoon, though, he was finished.

"You may go and see your friends," Mama told him, "but see you're back by supper."

"Aye!" Josiah assured her. But he didn't go to William's or Ezekiel's. Instead, he ran straight up the road toward Topsfield.

Hope was right about the widow's cabin. Someone was obviously living there, though whoever it was, was out at the moment. He saw the remains of a cooking fire in the tiny fireplace, and a few hard loaves of bread and a handful of turnips on the shelves. Josiah shook his head sadly as he ran his hand over the table. The widow would be ashamed to see this much dirt in her cabin. He and Hope had always tried to keep it as clean and cheerful as she had.

Josiah shivered as he moved around the cabin, looking for he wasn't quite sure what. There was a different feeling in here now as if someone mean must live here.

Josiah sat on one of the chairs. Whoever it was wouldn't live here long. He would wait until they came back and tell them just who this cabin belonged to.

He didn't have to wait long. Very soon he heard the rustling of branches and the lilt of girlish laughter. It didn't sound like the beggar woman's harsh, raspy voice, but he still expected a bent-over woman with stringy hair to appear when the door opened.

Instead, he found himself standing eye to eye with Abigail Williams and Ann Putnam.

They were as surprised as he was, because for a moment their faces froze, and Josiah thought he saw fear ripple through Ann's eyes.

But Abigail Williams didn't know about fear. As soon as she recovered, her eyes narrowed, her lip curled and she was on him.

"Josiah Hutchinson!" she said. "What are *you* doing here?"

"I might ask you the same question."

There was another surprised silence. Abigail broke it by laughing, but Josiah could see her watching him closely. Ann just stared.

"We discovered this place," she said, swishing past him. "And we come here sometimes. That's our food in the cupboards."

"Well, you'll have to move it out," Josiah said. "Because this place—this place belongs to—to—us."

"Says who?"

Josiah tilted his chin up. "The lady who lived here before."

Abigail put her hands on her hips as if she had him now.

"And was that that old Quaker woman you had living in your house for a time? Because if it was, she had no right to own property here anyway. My uncle says—"

"Your uncle's wrong."

Ann gasped.

"My uncle is the minister," Abigail said, lip curled almost to her nose. "How dare you—"

Josiah felt the anger stirring up inside him as he took a step toward Abigail. He wanted to be good and close so she didn't miss his next words.

But suddenly Abigail cowered, the way puppies did at the farm when a bigger dog came through. Snatching her skirts around her, she turned and ran—through the doorway, across the yard, and away.

Beside him, spidery little Ann Putnam cowered and screamed, "Don't strike me!"

Josiah stared at her. "I'm not going to strike you."

She peeked out at him through the hands she had thrown over her face. "You were going to strike Abigail!"

"I was not!"

"You looked as if you were!" she cried. And then she stood like a terrified rabbit, shaking and pulling away. It was a different experience for Josiah, being on this side of fear, but it wasn't hard to get used to.

"I want to ask you some questions," he said.

Ann nodded.

"Were you ever robbed on the Ipswich Road?"

Her arms flew out and she stepped back. "How did you know about that?"

"Joseph and I were robbed, too—well, almost robbed. I know that you—you ride your horse there often."

"Well, aye, I was, but I got away." Ann was beginning to recover some of her coldness, and she set her shoulders now.

"Do you know who it was tried to rob you?" Josiah asked.

"Aye—well, no—I saw his face because I pulled down his mask—but I didn't know him. Are you quite finished now, because I'm going—"

Josiah stepped into the doorway and blocked her path. She rolled her eyes, but she didn't try to push past him.

"So when you saw his face, he showed you his gold ring and tempted you with a gold chain to keep you from telling—and then when you and—and Abigail discovered this cabin—Hope was asleep here—and—and so Abigail made you put the chain—put the chain 'round her neck so she would get—get into trouble—instead of you. So my father would punish her for breaking the Puritan law about the wearing of fine jewelry—and you would get off free! After all—you couldn't have kept it hidden from your father much longer. You were bound to be caught with it sooner or later."

Ann Putnam's mouth fell open for a split second before she began to laugh. "Why would she do such a thing, Josiah Hutchinson?"

"Because Hope got her into trouble with her uncle—and because—because she's a wicked, spiteful girl!"

"Oh, is she now?" Ann said. "I think you're the spiteful one, to be making all of this up—"

"I saw the chain 'round *your* neck the day I saw you with Joseph Putnam," Josiah said quietly.

Ann bit her lip. Then she laughed again and gave Josiah's shoulder a shove.

He stepped back and let her go, because in that minute, he saw in her eyes that everything he'd said to her was true. He only needed to know one more thing.

"When you pulled off his mask," he called after her, "did the robber have red hair?"

"Aye—but so what?" Ann said. She picked up her skirts and turned to go. "You can't prove any of this, though, you brainless boy!" she said over her shoulder. "You have no proof at all!"

As she disappeared into the woods, Josiah had to admit that she was right.

✢ ✦ ✢

Chapter Sixteen

One night after supper, Papa brought out a set of wooden trenchers. Josiah fingered the initials his father had etched on them with his knife. "JPC," each trencher read.

"These are a wedding present for Joseph and Constance," Papa said.

"Aye, they're lovely," his wife said softly.

Josiah knew the J was for Joseph, the C for Constance, and the P for Putnam. His parents had some engraved trenchers, though not so fine as these.

"I've a notion to give them to them at the house-raising tomorrow," Papa said.

Josiah felt his face light up. It was the custom in Massachusetts in the 1690s for the community to come together to help a young couple about to be married to begin the building of their home.

"We'll be workin' dawn to dusk," Papa said. "It's to be a big, fine house."

"Am I to be allowed to go, Papa?" Hope said.

Josiah watched his father carefully. A house-raising was one of the few celebrations held in Puritan society. To miss a party might mean not going to one for another whole year. Maybe he should tell his father now what he suspected about the gold chain—what he knew was true—although without proof—

Papa studied his hands and began slowly to shake his head.

"Joseph."

Hope and Josiah turned quickly toward their soft-spoken mother.

She looked timidly at her husband, but her voice was sure. "It is for you to say, of course, but I see nothing to be gained by leavin' her at home."

That was all. She went back to scraping the trenchers.

"Good, then, let you come," Papa said to Hope. "But there's to be no talk of this chain business at the party, d'y'hear?"

Hope nodded. But Josiah kept his head very, very still. That wasn't something he wanted to agree to.

The property Joseph Putnam had inherited from his father was surely one of the best pieces of land in all of Salem, Village or Town. It sat high up on a hill to the west of the Ipswich River where the soil was rich and the brooks ran freely.

"I can imagine Constance Porter—*Putnam*—rocking her

babies by the window and looking down over her farm with
Joseph at her side," Sarah Proctor crooned the next afternoon as she, Rachel, and Hope sat with Ezekiel, William, and
Josiah on the grassy hillside. Josiah didn't know about that.
The whole idea of falling in love and marrying was still a
mystery to him. He could only think what a perfect place this
was for going to school and visiting his friend Joseph.

"Will you be eating that?" Ezekiel asked his sister Rachel,
his mouth stuffed and his finger pointing to the pile of
candied fruit she had left on her plate.

"In good time!" she snapped and pulled it out of his reach.

"You can have all of mine," Josiah said.

Ezekiel's eyes widened. Josiah still had a piece of mince
pie and half a slice of spice cake with maple sugar frosting on
his plate. He'd eaten enough sweets in Salem Town to last
him until Thanksgiving.

Ezekiel grabbed the cake and crammed it into his mouth.
The boys had worked up an appetite this morning, helping
their fathers raise the frame for Joseph Putnam's huge house.
This afternoon the men would nail the clapboards to protect
the house from rain while Joseph Putnam took his time finishing the inside. Ezekiel and William stretched out lazily on the
grass, but Josiah was restless, and his eyes wandered about
the crowd.

All the people he had expected would share in the party
were there—Israel Porter and his brood, all of the Proctors,
and several other families with whom the Hutchinsons were
friendly.

But Josiah was surprised when the "other" Putnams had

appeared. All of Joseph's halfbrothers—Thomas, Nathaniel, Edward, and John—and their families had arrived at mid-morning on horseback like a band of princes. Josiah's father had watched the men carefully as they took hold of boards and held them in place. *He is making sure they don't set a trap so a wall falls down,* Josiah thought.

Even the Reverend Parris had come and asked Joseph Putnam if he would like some prayers said over his land. Joseph was polite and everyone bowed their heads as the minister asked for God's blessings not only on the land but on the house they were about to build, and on the union that was about to be fixed between Joseph and Constance.

It occurred to Josiah as he prayed that Reverend Parris wasn't like the Putnams. He really did try to be a good person. Sometimes, he just got confused. Josiah understood how that felt.

As he looked over the crowd, Josiah's eyes snagged on another knot of girls. In the middle of them was Abigail Williams, and next to her sat Ann Putnam. Josiah remembered her last words to him. "You have no proof!" He'd thought about it so much since their meeting in the cabin. He was right about Simon and about her and the gold chain, but how could he make the others believe him? The proof—the proof—

"So, where is our proof, Josiah Hutchinson?"

Josiah jumped from his spot with a jerk. Ezekiel leered at him.

"Where is our proof?" he said again.

"Proof of what?" Josiah was still trying to peel his thoughts away from Ann Putnam.

"Proof that you went aboard a real ship." He nudged William. "Didn't we ask him to bring us proof?"

William nodded, but he didn't look at Josiah.

"I went aboard a ship," Josiah said. "Many times. I even sailed a bit on one—"

Ezekiel sprayed the air with his laughter. "You are a liar, Josiah!"

Josiah didn't say anything.

"So—if you were indeed on a ship—where is an anchor or a—a—"

He doesn't even know the names of things, Josiah thought. But he didn't put out any words for Ezekiel to grab. Nor did he tell them about the gold, jeweled boatswain's pipe in a drawer in the best room. His father had said he could keep it. He just looked at them.

"You," said Ezekiel, "are a liar."

"Believe as you wish," Josiah said simply. "You have my word. That should be enough."

Suddenly, William pointed. "You can ask him! Isn't that Phillip English?"

All heads turned as indeed the elegant Mr. English made his way across the land, with Mary at his side holding Hannah and coaxing Judith along beside her. Josiah's heart lifted. They were like his other family, and the sight of them made him want to race across the field.

But they were greeting Joseph Putnam and young Constance now, and Josiah held back.

"Go on, then, Ezekiel," Rachel said. "Ask him—if you dare."

The children all laughed—all except Josiah. His eye was caught by a figure who was following the English family. Josiah blinked to be sure, but there was no mistaking that head of red hair. Simon was here at Joseph Putnam's.

Josiah's head flipped around. Ann Putnam had seen Simon, too, and her tiny face had gone as white as goose feathers. He *was* right, after all. But the proof. The proof—

"Gather around, all!" Joseph Putnam shouted.

All the villagers left their grassy spots and their tables and formed a circle around Joseph Putnam and his soon-to-be-bride. The English family stood modestly beside them.

"My good friend Phillip English, from Salem Town," Joseph said.

There were polite murmuring and head-nodding. Josiah took his eyes off Simon long enough to notice that the Putnams were exchanging hot glances with each other. Simon hadn't noticed him yet, and Josiah tried to stay very still to keep it that way.

"Mr. English has brought us one of his strongest young workers from his wharf to help us finish off this house, gentlemen!" Joseph cried.

"No!"

It was only when the entire crowd turned their eyes on him that Josiah realized he was the one who had cried out. It had burst from him like a flame that couldn't be smothered.

"Josiah!" his father said.

"Don't let him come into your house, Joseph!" Josiah shouted now. "He'll rob you—he'll rob you blind!"

The crowd came alive with outraged chatter, but Josiah

could only look at Simon. The tall redhead stepped out from behind Phillip English, his eyes smoldering at Josiah with anger and hate. But Josiah whirled his head around the circle until he found Ann Putnam. Even from across the yard, he saw that she was trembling.

"Josiah!" his father said again. "Hush now!"

"Joseph, may I?" Phillip English said.

Joseph Hutchinson nodded, and Mr. English looked kindly at Josiah.

"Lad, I know that Simon here has caused you some problems aboard my ships. He made great trouble for you, especially that night out at sea, and I can appreciate your not trusting him. But it was you yourself who convinced me that perhaps Simon did some of the things he did because he had no one to care about him. Do you not agree that if given a chance—"

"No, sir." Josiah didn't shout this time, but the answer itself was enough to get the crowd going again.

Phillip English looked around helplessly, and Joseph Putnam stepped up beside him. "Go on, Josiah," he said. "Do you know something else?"

Josiah drew in a deep breath. Now was the time to help Hope. The chance might never come again.

"Aye," he said. "Simon is a robber. He steals from your own shop, Mr. English, on English's Lane. He tried to rob Joseph Putnam and me of all of my father's goods on the Ipswich Road." Josiah held his eyes on Joseph. "And he tried to rob Ann Putnam, too."

"What's this!" cried Thomas Putnam.

Heads wobbled from Thomas to Ann and back to Thomas.

In the midst of the confusion, Simon lunged across the crowd, straight at Josiah.

A raspy gurgle tore from Simon's throat as he let fly with his long, wiry arms and shoved Josiah to the ground. But there was no rolling and clawing and kicking this time. Almost before he'd fallen, Josiah was wrenched up by his father. Simon soon stood facing him, his arms pinned behind him by Phillip English.

"Who is this boy?" Joseph Hutchinson shouted.

"He's a thief, Papa!" In desperation, his eyes searched about Simon's waist. It was there! "Look into that pouch he wears! Look and see what's there!"

"That's your pouch, Josiah," whispered a voice beside him. Hope was at his elbow, her face the color of ashes.

Mr. English grabbed the pouch and jerked it from Simon's britches. He held it up for a second as if he recognized it, then he tumbled the contents into his hand. The crowd gasped as Phillip English held up a chunky ring made of gold with the letter S raised on it.

"What is it, Phillip?" Joseph Hutchinson asked.

"This was stolen from my shop several months ago! As were a number of other valuable—" His voice cut short, and he shook Simon roughly. "Are you the thief, boy?"

"Aye, he is!" Josiah said. "He wore that ring when he tried to rob Joseph Putnam and me. It dug into my arm when he grabbed me. It left its print on my skin."

"That's true, Phillip," Mary English said quietly. "I nursed the boy myself. I saw it."

An uncertain silence followed, as if even that were not

enough proof. Josiah opened his mouth once more.

"Ask Ann Putnam if she didn't see the ring when he tried to rob her," he said.

Heads swiveled toward Ann whose spidery face was pinched with terror. Her father looked down at her, his big face crimson. "You were never robbed!" His hand gave one of her frail arms a shake. "You were never robbed, and you never saw such a ring!"

Ann's eyes groped the crowd wildly, as if she were looking for someone, anyone, to tell her what to say. When they hit on Josiah, he nodded slowly. She stopped and her mouth began to move woodenly. "Aye, sir," she said in a thin voice. "I was— and it was this boy here who did it." She pointed at Simon.

"Traitor!" Simon screamed. It was more than just fear that cracked his voice. It was fury of a dangerous kind. Josiah had heard it before, and his heart quickened for Ann Putnam.

"You are a traitor!" Simon screamed again. "All right, then—tell them about the gold chain I gave you to shut your mouth, eh? Tell them of that!"

Another gasp rose up from the group, but none reacted so much as the Hutchinsons.

Hope grabbed Josiah's hand.

Ann searched the crowd again, but this time she found no help from Josiah. She tossed her almost-colorless blonde hair and said in a shaky voice, "What gold chain? I have no gold chain."

I saw it on you! Josiah was about to cry out. But another voice beat him to it.

"Gold chain?" Joseph Hutchinson said. He put his fingers

into his leather pouch and pulled out a shiny object. "This gold chain?"

It was Josiah's turn to catch his breath. The chain his father held up to the sun was exactly like the one he'd seen in Mr. English's shop. Exactly the kind Simon had stolen from there.

Slowly, Joseph Hutchinson crossed the circle and held out the chain to Ann Putnam. "This would seem to be yours, then. Now perhaps you should tell us how this got 'round my daughter's neck."

"Surely she stole it from my Ann!" Thomas Putnam cried.

Several people laughed, and Thomas Putnam's face reddened like a beet as he realized he had just as much as admitted that Ann indeed had had it at one time. Even his brother Edward nudged him and frowned.

Joseph Hutchinson's piercing eyes bored into Ann Putnam. "My daughter says she was asleep in Faith Hooker's cabin—"

"That Quaker again!" Nathaniel Putnam said.

Mr. Hutchinson cut him back with his eyes. "It is far less sinful to befriend a person of another faith than to bring shame on one of your own faith." All the Putnams shifted in their boots and were quiet. "The good widow left the cabin in the care of my children," Joseph Hutchinson went on, "and they go there oft times. When Hope awoke that day, she says she ran home. It wasn't until my wife saw the chain 'round her neck that she claims she noticed it, too."

"Are you accusing my daughter of going to some cabin to put this chain on your daughter?" Thomas laughed, looking at the crowd as if to get them to join in. But everyone was silent.

"I never knew of no cabin like that." Ann's voice was still thin and her face was white, but she was fighting hard.

"Yes, you do," Josiah said. "You came there just yesterday and claimed it was *your* cabin. You and Abigail Williams. You've left some of your things there."

Reverend Parris nearly shrieked as he grabbed hold of his niece. Hope squeezed Josiah's hand.

"It wasn't my doin'!" Ann Putnam suddenly cried out. "It was Abigail!"

Josiah thought Simon could deliver a look that would wither an ear of corn, but the one Abigail shot at her friend would wilt the entire crop. But Ann Putnam was grasping for any shred of hope to get her out of this, and Abigail was it. Hope and Josiah looked at each other and tried not to smile.

"You lie!" Abigail called back. "I never did no such thing!"

"You did! You bade me follow her that day. You made me give up the chain because you said it was a sin to wear it. You said Hope was deaf and would never hear us—!"

"Why would Abigail do such a thing?" Edward Putnam asked.

"Because she's a wicked, deceitful child—as are all of these!" cried the Reverend Parris. "They've not yet felt the hand of God on them; they have no conscience as yet—"

"I'm sorry, Reverend Parris," Joseph Hutchinson said in a quiet voice. "But, yet again, I must disagree with you." He looked at the two young Hutchinsons who stood beside him. "My two children have more of a conscience than many of the people standing right here on this land—and I am proud to say it. Hope—before this whole company of citizens, I will say it—I am sorry that I did not trust you at once. I should have known better."

Josiah felt the red climbing up into his cheeks, but for once it wasn't the red of shame. As he ducked his head from all the eyes that turned his way, he caught one pair that twinkled out at him. Without a sound, Joseph Putnam mouthed the words, "Aye, Captain."

‡ ⋅‡⋅ ‡

Chapter Seventeen

The end of summer always carried with it its own special magic in the Massachusetts colony. William and Ezekiel and Josiah were set free in the slow time before the fall harvest to gather berries in the woods, climb trees, and wade in the river. That summer of 1690, they even learned to prate for pigeons. Hiding in the tall grass and scrubby bushes, they imitated the chatter of the birds and lured them in for their fathers to shoot for the stews their wives would cook.

During one of those lazy summer afternoons, they were lying under a tree by the Ipswich River. All three of them had their boots off, and William kept watch for anyone approaching so they could quickly slip them on again.

Ezekiel was quiet, which was strange for him. Josiah just chewed on a long piece of grass and waited. The wheels inside Ezekiel's head were turning like the sawmill, and Josiah knew he'd soon churn something out.

Suddenly, Ezekiel flipped over onto his stomach and muttered, "I'm sorry."

"For what?" Josiah said.

"For not believing you when you said you'd been aboard Mr. English's ships and even sailed on one."

"Why do you believe me now?"

Ezekiel chewed on his lower lip. "Because Mr. English said you did when he was talking about that Simon boy and how much trouble he made for you. I'm sorry—I'm sorry I had to wait for someone else to prove it instead of believing you."

Josiah grinned. "I could hardly believe it myself. Sometime would you like to see my boatswain's pipe? It's gold and has jewels. Mr. English gave it to me."

Ezekiel's eyes widened, and he was too impressed even to ask what a boatswain's pipe was. "You can show me—I mean, I want to see it—but you don't have to prove to me—I was stupid to ask you to—"

Josiah laughed. "I know."

As the evenings grew cooler, many of the villagers went outside after supper and sat on their stoops, and neighbors came by to visit and drink cider. Josiah loved to pick up snatches of the grown-ups' conversations while he and Hope chased fireflies and frogs close by. The night Phillip English came to the village, Josiah sat as close as he could so as not to miss a word. Old Israel Porter joined them, and Mama even brought out some sweet cakes as a treat.

There was much talk about things like selectmen and timber for shipbuilding, and then all at once Mr. English turned to Josiah.

"I suppose you want to know what has happened to young Simon, eh?"

"Aye." Josiah's heart pounded at the sound of his name.

"I did think at first as you did, Josiah, that the boy needed a family, and I was willing to take him in. But I think you'll agree that it's going to take more than that to save him now." Phillip English shook his head sadly. "He was stealing my goods from my ships, my warehouse, my shops—even from my suppliers on the road, like your father!"

"What did he intend to do with it all?" Papa asked. "Surely he had no means to deal with it himself!"

Phillip's face grew dark. "He was selling the goods to Captain Hollingsworth. Simon didn't tell him where it came from—and it's sure Hollingsworth didn't ask. But surely he knew. Where else would he get such things, eh?"

Israel Porter nodded. "Hollingsworth is as much a thief as the boy, then, as I see it."

"Aye," Phillip English said. "But Hollingsworth gets no punishment. Simon does. He's spending his time with Reverend Nicholas Noyes while it's decided what should be done with him. There's no one to pay off his debts, and I'm surely not going to pawn so dishonest a lad off on some other seaman. What's to be done with him is not sure, but Reverend Noyes is looking for some relative."

"He has already suffered his worst punishment," Josiah said.

Everyone looked at him in surprise.

"What's that, son?" Papa asked.

"He won't be allowed to sail on the *Adventure* now, as he

was promised."

Mr. English's elegant eyebrows shot up. "He was never promised a voyage! Did he tell you that?"

"Aye."

"It was only a dream of his. Even before I knew he was a thief, I decided he would never make a sailor. He thought only of himself, that one. At sea, a man must be part of a team." His eyes softened as he looked at Josiah. "Now you, my good lad, would make a fine sailor—perhaps even an officer or ship's captain."

"I know nothing of the sea," Israel Porter said, "but I know you're right, Phillip. He's a good deal smarter than I ever gave him credit for, Joseph."

Papa just smiled and nodded.

Talk turned then to the wars with the Indians that were raging in Maine. Josiah didn't hear much of it. He was too busy enjoying the glow that was warming him all over.

Later that night, when he couldn't fall asleep, Josiah went to the window to catch the night breeze. It was a good thing Simon was caught, he thought, although no one seemed hopeful that he would ever be much better than he was now. Josiah sighed. He was glad he'd given him the scarf and let him keep the whistle pouch. He had nothing else now. Maybe knowing someone was kind to him would make a difference someday. Maybe—

"I never thanked you properly." Hope had padded silently from her bed and was beside him now at the window.

"For what?" Josiah said.

"For clearing my name over the gold chain. And I've decided you need a reward."

She pulled her hand from behind her back and opened it in front of him. A piece of white linen unfolded on her palm.

When Josiah picked it up, a red ribbon that served as a drawstring fell across his fingers. It was a whistle pouch, and from the tiny stitches, Josiah knew she had made it herself.

"Perhaps this one will bring you better fortune, eh?" she said.

Josiah grinned, and then his eye caught the corner of the bag. There in shining red stitches were four letters: JJHC.

Josiah Joseph Hutchinson.

He looked quizzically at his sister. "C?"

"Captain," she whispered.

Josiah ducked his head and felt his cheeks turn red. He never knew what to say when things like this happened. In front of him, Hope laughed softly, and poked at his leg with her toe.

"Now then, what were you thinking when I caught you sitting here?"

"You'll think it silly," he said.

"I won't."

Josiah waggled his shoulders. "I was thinkin' of Simon. Feelin' sorry for him."

"I don't think that's silly at all. I feel sorry for Abigail Williams—how's that for silly?"

"Because she has no parents?" Josiah said.

"Aye. And because she lives in a house where people are afraid to learn new things and change their way of thinking.

That's what Papa says. He says God can't do His work when people are so closed up." She looked at Josiah seriously. "I'm of a mind to try and make friends with Abigail. What say you to that?"

"I say you're brave!"

Hope sighed and looked out the window and down on Salem Village, sleeping below them. Josiah thought he saw the shine of tears in her eyes. "So many things are changing, Josiah. Papa says the fighting with the Indians is terrible in Maine, and that soon men from this very village will go off to war. Sergeant Thomas Putnam has already started drilling some on the training field. Papa's worried about his brother-in-law—Uncle Daniel."

"Who's that?"

"Husband to his sister Esther."

Josiah had never met his aunt and uncle, and their names came to him now like distant memories he'd tucked away.

"Other things are changing, too," Hope said. "You'll be spendin' more time on your schooling with Joseph Putnam. Papa's planting fewer crops next year. And I don't suppose we'll be going to the cabin anymore."

Josiah had thought that, too, and he nodded. "It used to be a secret place for us."

"I don't suppose Abigail and Ann will be going there anymore, either, but if it isn't secret and special, something's gone out of it."

Josiah agreed. "But should we let it fall to ruin? We always thought the widow left it for us."

Hope cocked her head. "I've thought on that, Josiah. What

say you if we found that beggar woman we met that day—the one who came stormin' up to the cabin when we were all there?"

"Aye."

"What say you if we find her and let her stay in the cabin. She has nowhere to live, and since we can't help Simon or Abigail or Uncle Daniel—"

Her voice trailed off sadly, and Josiah's nod was sad, too. It was a good thing to do, but a sad one, all at once. He'd discovered that happened a great deal.

But suddenly, he lifted his chin at Hope. "All change doesn't have to be bad, y'know," he said to her.

Her face wrinkled into a question.

"You have earned Papa's trust back again," he said. "That's a good change. And I've learned to read. And we've Joseph Putnam for a friend now."

He stopped. Hope looked at him closely, and she looked for so long that he turned his head away, cheeks glowing red.

"I see another change," she said. "Something has caught my eye these last few days."

"What?" Josiah looked down at his hands and fiddled with them.

"I've noticed that you hardly ever stutter anymore. And you don't hang your head like a whipped dog, either. Did you know it?"

He did know it, and he smiled up at Hope as he nodded.

"Perhaps it's all right then," she went on, "that so many old things are ending."

Josiah looked down on the sleepy village and smiled. "Aye.

With all of those things ending, better things are beginning. And do you know why?"

"Nay."

"Because—we've both proven that we can be trusted. Eh?"

Hope leaned against the window, crossed her arms, and narrowed her eyes at him. They glistened in the moonlight. "You tell me something, Josiah, and you tell me now." She leaned in for the question. "How did my silly little brother get to be so smart?"

Josiah shrugged, but he knew the answer. God, of course, was the Smart One. He'd just waited for Josiah to ask the right questions.

✢ ⚜ ✢

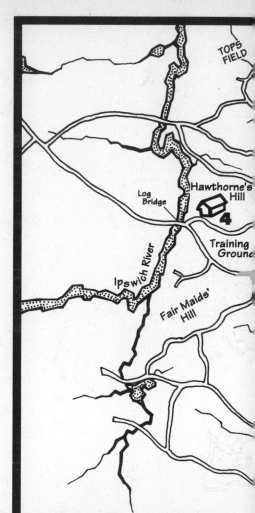

1. Lt. John Putnam
2. Widow's Cabin
3. Joseph Putnam
4. Sgt. Putnam
5. Capt. Walcott
6. Rev. Parris
7. Meeting House
8. Nathan Ingersoll
9. Nathaniel Putnam
10. Israel Porter
11. Dr. Griggs
12. John Porter's Mill
13. John & Elizabeth Proctor

A Map of
SALEM VILLAGE
& Vicinity in 1692

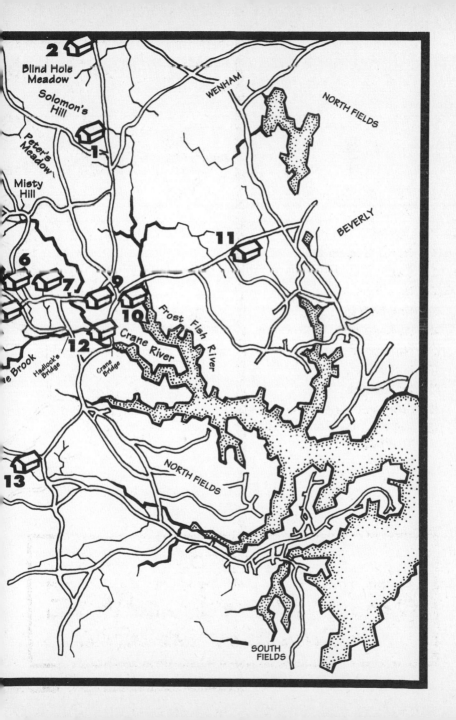

There's More Adventure in the CHRISTIAN HERITAGE SERIES!

The Salem Years, 1689–1691

The Rescue #1

Josiah Hutchinson's sister Hope is terribly ill. Can a stranger—whose presence could destroy the family's relationship with everyone else in Salem Village—save her?

The Stowaway #2

Josiah's dream of becoming a sailor seems within reach. But will the evil schemes of a tough orphan named Simon land Josiah and his sister in a heap of trouble?

The Guardian #3

Josiah has a plan to deal with the wolves threatening the town. Can he carry it out without endangering himself—or Cousin Rebecca, who'll follow him anywhere?

The Accused #4

Robbed by the cruel Putnam brothers, Josiah suddenly finds himself on trial for crimes he didn't commit. Can he convince anyone of his innocence?

The Samaritan #5

Josiah tries to help a starving widow and her daughter. But will his feud with the Putnams wreck everything he's worked for?

The Secret #6

If Papa finds out who Hope's been sneaking away to see, he'll be furious! Josiah knows her secret; should he tell?

The Williamsburg Years, 1780–1781

The Rebel #1

Josiah's great-grandson, Thomas Hutchinson, didn't rob the apothecary shop where he works. So why does he wind up in jail, and will he ever get out?

The Thief #2

Someone's stealing horses in Williamsburg! But is the masked rider Josiah sees the real culprit, and who's behind the mask?

The Burden #3

Thomas knows secrets he can't share. So what can he do when a crazed Walter Clark holds him at gunpoint over a secret he doesn't even know?

The Prisoner #4

As war rages in Williamsburg, Thomas' mentor refuses to fight and is carried off by the Patriots. Now which side will Thomas choose?

The Invasion #5

Word comes that Benedict Arnold and his men are ransacking plantations. Can Thomas and his family protect their homestead—even when it's invaded by British soldiers who take Caroline as a hostage?

The Battle #6

Thomas is surrounded by war! Can he tackle still another fight, taking orders from a woman he doesn't like—and being forbidden to talk about his missing brother?

The Charleston Years, 1860–1861

The Misfit #1

When the crusade to abolish slavery reaches full swing, Thomas Hutchinson's great-grandson Austin is sent to live with slave-holding relatives. How can he ever fit in?

The Ally #2

Austin resolves to teach young slave Henry-James to read, even though it's illegal. If Uncle Drayton finds out, will both boys pay the ultimate price?

The Threat #3

Trouble follows Austin to Uncle Drayton's vacation home. Who are those two men Austin hears scheming against his uncle—and why is a young man tampering with the family stagecoach?

The Trap #4

Austin's slave friend Henry-James beats hired hand Narvel in a wrestling match. Will Narvel get the revenge he seeks by picking fights and trapping Austin in a water well?

The Hostage #5

As north and south move toward civil war, Austin is kidnapped by men determined to stop his father from preaching against slavery. Can he escape?

The Escape #6

With the Civil War breaking out, Austin tries to keep Uncle Drayton from selling Henry-James at the slave auction. Will it work, and can Austin flee South Carolina with the rest of the Hutchinsons before Confederate soldiers find them?

The Chicago Years, 1928–1929

The Trick #1

> Rudy and Hildy Helen Hutchinson and their father move to Chicago to live with their rich great-aunt Gussie. Can they survive the bullies they find—not to mention Little Al, a young schemer with hopes of becoming a mobster?

The Chase #2

> Rudy and his family face one problem after another—including an accident that sends Rudy to the doctor, and the disappearance of Little Al. But can they make it through a deadly dispute between the mob and the Ku Klux Klan?

The Capture #3

> It's Christmastime, but Rudy finds nothing to celebrate. Will his attorney father's defense of a Jewish boy accused of murder—and Hildy Helen's kidnapping—ruin far more than the holiday?

The Stunt #4

> Rudy gets in trouble wing-walking on a plane. But can he stay standing as he finds himself in the middle of a battle for racial equality— and Aunt Gussie's dangerous fight for workers' rights?

Available at a Christian bookstore near you

FOCUS ON THE FAMILY®

Like this book?

Then you'll love *Clubhouse* magazine! It's written for kids just like you, and it's loaded with great stories, interesting articles, puzzles, games, and fun things for you to do. Some issues include posters, too! With your parents' permission, we'll even send you a complimentary copy.

Simply write to Focus on the Family, Colorado Springs, CO 80995 (in Canada, write P.O. 9800, Stn. Terminal, Vancouver, B.C. V6B 4G3) and mention that you saw this offer in the back of this book. Or, call 1-800-A-FAMILY (in Canada, call 1-800-661-9800).

You may also visit our Web site (www.family.org) to learn more about the ministry or find out if there is a Focus on the Family office in your country.

• • •

"Adventures in Odyssey" is a fantastic series of books, videos, and radio dramas that's fun for the entire family—parents, too! You'll love the twists and turns found in the novels, as well as the excitement packed into every video. And the 30 albums of radio dramas (available on audiocassette or compact disc) are great to listen to in the car, after dinner . . . even at bedtime! You can hear "Adventures in Odyssey" on the radio, too. Call Focus on the Family for a listing of local stations airing these programs or to request any of the "Adventures in Odyssey" resources. They're also available at Christian bookstores everywhere.

Focus on the Family is an organization that is dedicated to helping you and your family establish lasting, loving relationships with each other and the Lord. It's why we exist! If we can assist you or your family in any way, please feel free to contact us. We'd love to hear from you!